Piper's Plan
Clearwater Daddies
Book 1
Alyssa Bailey

Description of Piper's Plan

Piper has awesome plans, but they defy Daddy's rules. Things could get hot.

Piper Gentry was not one to back down from a challenge, not in her international investments company or in her personal life. Piper looks for sense in her father's death while looking for ways to make the family ranch profitable again in the wild heat of a Texas summer.

Jackson Knight has always loved Piper Gentry. Being her husband and Daddy, raising their family on the ranch is all he has ever wanted, but she never returned from college. Now she's back and his challenge is to remind her that his plans are still her plans and that she feels the same about him. He'll stop at nothing to keep her near him and safe.

Piper's plan does not involve taking orders from anyone, including Jackson, but her longing for what they once had, has her doubting herself. Who will pose the greatest threat to her safety—outsiders eager to get their hands on her family legacy, or Piper herself?

Chapter 1

Jackson's deep royal-blue eyes stared hard at the appropriately overcast sky. The sun's previously valiant efforts at pushing past the cloud cover seemed a victory unnecessary today. The somber gathering of nearly forty people stood at the graveside of Garth Gentry.

Jackson flattened his dark hair down after taking off his dress Stetson and resettled the impressive hat on his head. His brothers, Walker and Sawyer Knight, stood next to him as well as their foreman Cody Race, paying their respects and representing the rest of the Clear Knight Ranch.

The Knight brothers were a striking trio. Walker, the eldest with his chocolate brown hair and brown eyes, Jackson with his almost black hair and intensely blue eyes, and Sawyer with his crystal bright blue eyes and blonde hair. The brothers stood over six feet tall and were each solid as a rock. Their personalities matched their coloring.

Jackson was the more serious-minded brother with a cautious, demanding way about him. Walker, the most mellow brother, often was the voice of reason. Sawyer was the brother who reacted first, and asked questions later. He was willing to try anything once, and often did.

Jackson looked over at the Gentry family, and his heart went out to them. His eyes naturally sought out Piper Gentry, the girl and later young woman who had stolen his heart forever. Just at that moment, she lifted her sorrow-filled smoky-dark hazel gaze. Those eyes could be as cold and hard as ice or as hot and smokey as a burning field in the spring. His chest seized in love, with an overwhelming desire to hold her while kissing her tears away, as he'd done once upon a time.

Regret for allowing her to stay gone for so long, ate at him. There were reasons why he'd made the choices he did but he was older and didn't give a shit what others wanted or thought. She was his. Had always been his and now was the time to claim what was his and declare that ownership to the world. Time they went on with the rest of their life.

This was the first sight of Piper he'd gotten since she returned home almost a week ago. Had his girl been too overcome with grief? Likely. Was she avoiding him? Definitely. He focused on her little girl lost signals she mournfully sent him and he couldn't resist taking care of his baby.

Instinctively, he started to walk over to draw her to him when Sawyer grabbed his forearm and nodded his head in the direction of the minister. Oh, right, he was going to say a few words. He inclined his head in understanding and took one last look in Piper's direction before turning to stride forward to stand next to the minister. Jackson tried not to focus only on Piper, but it was to her that he spoke.

"My earliest memory of Garth Gentry was when I was a small boy. He helped a foolish young man down from a tree I never should have been climbing. And he never told my dad, which saved me a hot seat and earned him a spot nearly as high as my father's." There were smiles and subdued chuckles, as he'd hoped. "In all the years that followed he never fell from that pedestal. Our families helped each other over the years and he spoke just fifteen months ago when my brothers and I were mourning our own father." Jackson said a few more words before ending with, "Rafe, Rosie, Piper, if you need anything just call the house. My brothers and I would be honored to continue our ranch's tradition of friends as close as family."

Jackson walked away from the minister who soon closed the service just as he reached Piper.

Jackson leaned down to whispered in her ear. "Piper darlin', I'm so sorry."

She turned and looked up at him. She hiccupped a stifled cry turning toward Jackson. Her hazel eyes were red-rimmed and watery with shifting emotions evident on her face and showing her hesitancy. Suddenly, she let go a great sob and fell into his arms, weeping on his western shirt-covered chest.

His arms wrapped securely around her as he gently rocked her in comfort, murmuring soothing words. He had done this so many times over the years. It was almost as though time had stood still since the last time he was in this role. He kissed her head and smoothed her hair inhaling her lilac scented sweetness.

After a few more moments, Piper pulled away and started bringing herself back into some kind of order, brushing nonexistent wrinkles from her black pant suit and placing a few strands of her hair behind her ear as she took another step away from Jack's sheltering arms.

She looked up at him sheepishly, giving him a watery smile. "Thank you. I'd better take my place beside the rest of the family."

He reached out to touch her, already feeling the loss of her presence. "I'll come by later to see you, if that's all right?" He added the nicety even though he intended to come regardless of her response. Yeah, he could be an asshole sometimes but he intended to be that man she called on every time.

Piper nodded and smiled wanly. "Tomorrow?"

He nodded as he watched her return to her siblings. Tomorrow would work. The only Gentrys left in the ranching community were Piper's family. He observed how she straightened her spine and took measured steps with a great show of control. If you hadn't seen the breakdown, you would never have known it'd happened.

Tomorrow, baby cakes. You are mine and we will start again tomorrow. Daddy's going to take care of you.

Service over, Jackson jumped in the truck where his brothers and Cody were waiting. It was quiet for a moment before Walker said, "Well, she looks just as she did last time, but things are different. Is she more subdued? Somber?"

Jackson nodded. "Older."

No one needed to identify who she was. They all knew Jackson was in love with Piper. That she was his baby girl and he was her daddy. They also knew he was devastated when she didn't return home after college. What they didn't know is why he didn't go after her. No matter how much his family had tried to find another woman to take her place, to turn his head, it was to no avail. She would always be his and he would always be hers.

Today, Jackson felt frustrated and confused with his emotions churning up the old heartache again. He had expected to realize he was holding a candle for a woman that he no longer felt things for. A candle he thought he would be able to snuff out, finally.

That had changed when she accepted his comfort without reserve. He was going to put things back the way they should have been all along. He would get her back. Spank that delectable ass for putting them both through so much heartache, and then he was going to tie her to him for the rest of their natural lives.

"How do you think Garth Gentry died, anyway?" asked Walker.

"No telling. Probably a heart attack. No, wait, I think the obituary said an accident," recalled Sawyer.

"Wow, plenty of those on a ranch, but he was a cautious man. Such a waste," said Cody, the manager of Clear Knight Ranch.

They drove past the Gentry place on their way home. Sawyer, the fair-haired youngest of the three, asked the question they had all been wondering.

"So, what do you think they're going to do with Garth's place now?"

While Jackson had been the closest to Garth Gentry, their manager Cody was buddies with Andy, manager of the Gentry ranch. "Andy says it's anybody's guess," said Cody. "Rosie lives in Italy so unless her husband is moving, she won't stay. Rafe, he always tolerated the place, but he has bigger plans with his journalism career." He stopped and turned to Jackson. "Now your girl is the dark horse. Andy says she loves the *place*, but you couldn't tell it by me. She hardly ever came up more than a weekend."

Jackson grunted. "Well, don't look at me. I don't know her as well as I used to, but one thing hasn't changed. If Piper Gentry wants something, she'll move heaven and earth to get it."

"Well, brother of mine, looks like there are several good reasons for you to get reacquainted with our Miss Piper. That land developer will be sniffing around again in no time flat as soon as he knows Garth has passed on. We need to get our foot in the door, so they sell to us if they're going to sell." Walker looked at Jackson through the rearview mirror.

Sawyer slapped him on the shoulder. "Now you have several reasons to talk to her. Don't waste them."

GARTH GENTRY'S children trudged back through the front door of the home they'd grown up in, all now dealing with various stages of grief. Rosie decided to go and lie down to try to relieve the pounding headache that she acquired after the memorial. She missed her husband more than she had thought possible.

Rafe went ahead and put in a call to his girlfriend hoping to relieve some of the tension by listening to her bubbly conversation.

Piper tried to push away the thought that the woman was probably so perky because that's all she had were bubbles in her head. She appropriately bit her tongue and went into the kitchen to peer out the window at the rolling hills in the back of the house.

After standing there, allowing her thoughts to ramble to nowhere in particular, Piper decided she'd like to saddle up and go for a ride where there wasn't anyone to bother her and she could simply exist in the vastness of the ranch. She had so many things she needed to think about, not only pertaining to the multitude of decisions they needed to make about the ranch, but the next stage of her business and even her own substantially lacking private life.

Piper received a call late yesterday that she refused to answer because it wasn't something she wanted to deal with yet. Staving off the last of her headache was the excuse she told herself so she didn't have to deal with the inevitable which would come sooner rather than later. There was an undeniable knot in the pit of her stomach warning her of dramatic changes in the wind. Piper wasn't good with change she didn't initiate. Pops wasn't supposed to die yet.

Piper looked around the food-laden table and counters in the big farm kitchen her mother had loved. The neighbors left food to help them through the horrific days following their father's funeral. It was something people in this ranching community did for each other. Her parents had done it for others, and it had been gladly reciprocated.

However, now that all the friends and other family members had left, being at the ranch seemed awkward. It had been a long time since the Gentry kids had all been together. It was the first time without a parent. The first time they were alone.

Rosie came back into the kitchen giving Piper a wry smile and a shrug. "I couldn't settle down to rest."

"Do you two remember the last time we were all together?" Piper asked as she looked up to see Rafe entering the room.

"Well," said Rosie, "it's just over a year since you and I were here last, but Rafe was gone then."

"Right, I was out of the country."

"Rafe, you're always traveling somewhere," said Rosie.

Piper continued. "Now, if I remember right, I was here that Christmas. I had just done an acquisition. I'd burnt out and needed a rest."

Rafe chuckled. "So no news there."

Piper shot him a scathing look and then spoke to Rosie again. "It was when you got married, Rosie."

"Yes, yes, you're right. I remember. Mama wouldn't travel to Italy, so we had to have the big wedding in Italy because Tony has an enormous family. And then a smaller one with a reception here."

The room grew silent after the mention of their mother. Each took a seat in quiet remembrance. She had passed away not two months after Rosie's wedding. An aneurysm had taken Janine Gentry suddenly after their father had gone out to work on the ranch. She had been feeling off but that wasn't unusual in the last year of her life. It was Dawn, their house helper's day off, so it was several hours before Garth had found the love of his life on the floor.

"Pops was never the same after that." Piper stifled a sob. "And now he's gone, too."

The trio scooted their chairs closer to comfort one another. Soon Rafe stood, slapping his hands on his thighs as he did when he made a decision.

"Okay, let's take our glasses and some of this dessert we have everywhere and sit in the family room."

Rafe liked to take charge. The girls didn't mind. They ruled their own worlds quite well enough so could allow him that little joy. Still, they would miss Garth's voice taking the lead in family things. They reminisced for the rest of the evening before entering their old rooms and falling onto their childhood beds. Exhaustion giving them blessed sleep.

Chapter 2

The next morning came late as each of the siblings got up at their leisure.

"Rosie, do you get to sleep in all the time?"

"Time is so different. I'm used to getting up when you are going to bed and going to bed when the ranch is cooking dinner or earlier. I do get up to make Tony breakfast."

"What? You make breakfast and he eats it?" asked Piper.

"Is that why he isn't here?" teased Rafe.

"Stop it. I can cook pretty well, now. I'll be honest, though, it was hard learning in a new country with a different language. But I also learned you can figure out how to do anything for love."

Piper sighed. That was it, wasn't it? She hadn't tried hard enough to keep her own love when she had him, and she'd lost him. Yes, yesterday he was kind, but she'd not been his to protect, and so he left her there. When they were together, he would never have done that. He'd have taken her home, stayed with her and been here today taking care of necessities regardless of her words. He never would have let go of her hand. He hadn't back then. It had been she who'd let go first.

She'd walked away like a coward, without a word, years ago. She'd kept Jackson Knight in her heart because he was there standing in the way of every man she could have loved, waiting for her to love him back. Piper was doomed to a life of longing for a man who led a different life. One who took his ranching and breeding business as seriously as she took her investments.

It wasn't the commute, although it was quite a distance, but it had been their chosen lifestyles that kept them distant. And her. Really, if there was any fault to be had with two very young adults ended a special bond, it had been hers to own. She'd hurt him. She hadn't understood how much until she matured and had gone looking for that elusive connection and discovered she already had one that she couldn't sever. Maybe she didn't want to sever it.

Piper did a mental headshake. *If I hadn't left, I wouldn't be successful, respected, or wealthy enough to retire at thirty.* The cupid on her other shoulder reminded her she was alone and lonely, with no one to share it with. Her prospects were many, but she still loved Jackson, for all the good it would do her. He'd moved on. He had to have. She wondered what type of woman had scored that man.

With a sigh she realized, she'd do what she always did. She would take care of business and move on to the next challenge. This time she would shake Jackson off and find a man who would satisfy her longings, without tying her to a ranch that she loved but would never bring her what she had now. People listened to her, took note of her opinion.

The cupid Piper whispered in her ear that she had all of that and was still empty inside. Maybe it was time to look in a new direction. She kicked the weak, needy hearts and roses Piper aside and shoved the stronger, assertive devil Piper out front. No more time to long for unrealized dreams to come true.

She was a businesswoman and time to get down to business. Assess the situation, research the options, work viable plans, decide the best one, and charge forward. It had always worked for her in business. It would work in her personal life. Piper was thorough. She was successful. She was desperate for permanence.

Piper looked at her siblings. "Okay then, right after breakfast, I'm going to start working in the office and find out what there is to find. Rafe, do you think you could take a walk around with Andy today to see what Dad has for inventory? Help figure out what needs to be repaired, replaced, in order of the importance. That would be great. Take note of anything you feel is something we should know. I'll look for an inventory sheet."

"Good idea." Rafe nodded as though he let her take charge often. In fact, she didn't think he had ever allowed it before this moment. They had indeed grown up. "We should bring Andy in on the discussion afterward as well. He's going to be the best resource for us."

"I agree. And Rosie if you could do the same for the house that would be great. I know it's going to be difficult for all of us but the sooner the better. Check the storeroom too, please."

Piper gathered her sister in a bear hug as they shared a quick cry before standing to tackle the tasks. Piper had always been the natural leader of any group or project she was participating in, and she was glad her siblings did not take offense. Others would part the way because of the efficient, confident manner she had. Her siblings, not so much.

Her family had been different. Her family tolerated her, but the men were happily given the lead. She'd always been the youngest whom they tried to shelter. Even now, she lived on bravado sometimes, bluffing her way to the point of assured success. That worked for everyone except Jackson. Jackson gave her the lead until she was over her head and then he would step in to take over, sometimes yanking the reins from her fully engaged hands.

If she didn't yield the control, he... Her mind stuttered at the sudden reminder of why she had hesitated to continue her relationship with Jackson. How could she have forgotten? No, she had pushed it out of her mind so that she didn't have to deal with it. She'd left because she'd been young, full of herself, scared she would be lost at the ranch, and Jackson Knight was a spanker. A daddy. He spanked in sex, which was hot as hell, but he didn't stop there. He spanked as a tool for discipline and while he was protective and possessive, he was also stern.

She smiled, he'd had to be at times or she would have run circles around him. Sometimes she did anyway, but it was always because he indulged her. And he babied her, pushed her, encouraged her...loved her. Piper shuddered as she remembered her love-hate relationship with that Jackson reality.

Coming back from college, Piper was smart, independent, and full of ideas on how to make her mark in the world outside of the ranch. She didn't need a daddy. She needed a partner and she was too young and inexperienced to know she could have both.

Jackson had come back with plenty of ideas on how to make his mark in the world while living on the ranch. Piper had built her investment company with a manner that engendered trust using intellectual sweat equity, some sound investments and pure luck at times, bringing it into international circles. Jackson had moved into breeding and training, also taking him into an international realm.

Both successful and well known in their fields of expertise. Both driven in their life goals, but she was lacking in her personal life. She wondered who Jackson had decided on as his life partner. After a few pity party moments, she resolutely redirected herself. Pushing all thoughts of Jackson out of her mind, she strode toward the office her father had sat in nearly every evening of his life.

Preparing mentally for the arduous task of signing into her father's computer without his password, she was surprised that after firing up the older version of technology, that he didn't have a password on any of his work. Odd, for a man who was meticulous about locking up his logbooks and inventories that he still kept on paper, to leave all his precious computer files open and vulnerable.

"Why would he leave it unprotected?" she spoke aloud to no one and was startled when she got a response back.

"Who did he need to protect it from?" answered the deep, melodic voice of her most enduring source of longing.

"Jackson." She leaned back in her father's chair, good for a man his size, but overly large for a woman of hers. She craned her neck lock her eyes on him. Her heart picked up it's rhythmic beat and damn if she didn't squeeze her thighs together to stifle the tingle there. Some days she could use a daddy like the one in front of her but it wasn't a road she could go down now.

"I forgot how tall you are."

His bark of laughter eased the initial tension. "And you are as petite as ever."

She unconsciously sat up in her chair. "I'm average height."

He nodded and took another step into the office. "Yes, you are Miss Honeybun."

She shook her dark blonde waves. "Don't call me that. We did that as kids. I don't even eat those anymore," she said, thinking of the unnatural number of them she had consumed growing up.

There was a pause in the room as though he was choosing his words carefully. Piper found she'd held her breath until he spoke again. "*Honey* still okay?"

"I-I guess, but not in public. You know, with people we don't know. Besides, what's wrong with my name?"

"Pips?" he shrugged. "I guess I thought you wouldn't want me using that since it was short for Pipsqueak." His smile grew to irritating proportions.

"Of course not, I mean... right... not that but my *real* name." She felt her cheeks warm in her flustered state, angry her body was responding in the way it always had, arousal ignited.

"Sorry. I'll try to be careful. And nothing is wrong with Piper. I just love endearments when it comes to you. I want to cuddle you every time I see you, so using cuddle words make me happy."

Piper looked into his earnest blue eyes. She missed those eyes. Jackson abruptly sat in one of the chairs in front of the large, solid oak rancher's desk. Leaning back, he crossed one leg over the other and put his hat on his propped boot tip speaking casually, as though they did this every day.

"So, baby, what happens now?"

Piper sighed. "Well, we look at everything and then decide what we need to do. Suggestions?"

"Don't know yet. I'd say do your inventory. Afterward, I could bring over Cody to help Andy and y'all tease things out." This was the man she could work with. The business Jackson.

"That sounds good. We could use all the good ranching sense available. Jackson?"

"Mm hm."

"We might find we need to sell."

She spoke the words gently, hoping to ease the impact. She knew how much Jackson loved her father and this ranch. I wouldn't want them to sell. Jack's hand paused from running over the rim of his hat for just a split second before continuing.

"Well, I'd say we cross that bridge when we get to it. Until then, let's not borrow trouble."

"Good, okay, I just needed to say it."

He nodded and stood. "Got a customer coming by soon so I ought to get going. You let me know if you need help and call me when you're ready to talk about... things."

"About the ranch, I will."

"And other things." He leaned over and gently kissed her unsuspecting lips, before turning to walk out of the office.

Damn. That man did it again with a look, a word, and a kiss. She was not prepared for an emotional tangle right now and not with Jackson. She played to win but he had already stacked the deck in his favor. Losing wasn't always a bad thing, right? And would he have kissed her if he had a woman at home? No, she knew without a doubt, his morals wouldn't allow that. She got back to work before she went down a rabbit trail she would never return from unscathed.

A few days later, the Gentry and Knight siblings along with managers Cody and Andy were sitting around the large dinner table catching up and discussing the ranches.

"So how is it living in Italy, Rosie?" asked Sawyer as he lifted his forkful of corn soufflé no one at the table knew how to make. Thank goodness for neighbors.

"I love it, mostly. I miss the life here sometimes, but Tony is so good to me, I could never complain. It hurt him that he couldn't come, but it's the beginning of tourist season for him, and that's where we make the most money." She shrugged in a characteristically Italian way. "And the weather is incredible."

"But you'll tell him we miss him," added Piper.

"And Rafe, I hear you're moving up in the world of journalism," said Walker as he accepted more coffee from Rosie.

Rafe turned his full attention to Walker. "I love being a reporter, but want to move from newspaper to more correspondent work. That's what my next assignment is. In fact, I fly out of the country for several months next week, so things here need to be in a semi settled state by then. And honestly," he sought his sister's face, "now that Dad's gone, I don't really have a reason to come back. Ranching and country living is great to grow up in but not my thing now."

Piper redirected the group. "Let's take dessert and this conversation into the family room, where we can settle in."

Piper walked into the office to gather her paperwork. Concentrating, she turned, colliding into a hard, masculine chest. She would know the arms that came out to steady her anywhere. The combined scent of his particular musk combined with freshly showered Jackson was uniquely his. As it wafted past her nose, it tantalized, eliciting a familiar but long absent tingle in response. Twice in a few days was more than she'd been aroused in a year.

She gazed up in time to see his head descending toward hers, blocking all but the reality of his lips taking possession of hers. The welcomed sweetness drew an unbidden moan from deep within her soul. She'd missed this—him —and would never get enough. His lips caressed as his tongue sought the moist warmth of her mouth.

"Open for me baby, such a good Daddy's girl," he murmured.

She complied without thinking, whimpering as she battled for supremacy in the war of tongues. Her breath became shallow and labored. Jackson matched her breathing efforts as he pulled away, leaning his forehead on hers.

"Fuck. That was incredible," he rasped. "I've missed this so damn much."

She shook her head and whispered, "Please, I don't know if I can."

"What can't you do, baby?"

"This. With you. The Daddy gig, the protector, possessor, emotional connection. I don't know if I can give enough to it."

"But you want to. Piper, baby you need boundaries, protection, possession. You need this Daddy to claim you. It has nothing to do with can you do it, but can you do without it for any longer?"

"Damn it, you always make your case quickly."

She tried to turn away but he stalled her and instead laid his forehead on hers.

"Piper, I want you more than I have ever wanted a woman ever. Ever. Let me show you how good this could be with us."

"Oh, sorry," said Rafe.

Piper tried to pull away, but Jackson made her wait by tightening his arms around her waist. He dropped one more kiss before releasing and turning to face Rafe.

"No problem. We were on our way," smiled Jackson as he stepped back to allow Piper to walk in front of him.

He placed his hand on the small of her back and she felt the gentle pressure he exerted as he followed her and Rafe into the family room. She was grateful her legs held her up, but she had a feeling Jackson was there partly to make sure she didn't stumble.

She watched as he strode into the kitchen after she'd sat in the loveseat. The screen door slammed a few seconds later. She knew he needed a few minutes to compose himself. She stifled the smile that teased her lips. He was likely trying to calm his dick down and get his libido under control. She wished she had that luxury.

"Where's he going?" asked Sawyer.

"Probably to get some air," answered Rafe, looking hard in the direction of the kitchen.

"Huh," replied Walker.

"Well, let's get this started," said Rafe. "It'll take all night if we don't."

"Maybe I should grab Jackson." Walker stood up.

"No," sang the triple response from Rafe, Sawyer, and Piper.

Walker raised his eyebrows but said nothing and sat back down. She knew Jackson would get an earful later.

Rafe started with his information, and let Andy take over on the equipment and the other work needed. Andy threw out an estimate that had the men whistling and reaching for more coffee.

"And that is if we don't do any upgrades. I don't think we can get away without some of them. Some equipment isn't worth fixing."

Then came Rosie's information. "The house is solid and other than a few areas of dry rot that we can easily repair, I don't see any issues on the surface. Nothing consistent use and some TLC won't cure that is. Here's an active inventory of supplies on hand. Dad didn't need much, and he didn't have a garden since mom passed."

Somewhere during the talking, Jackson had walked in to sit quietly next to Piper on the loveseat. She smiled at the irony that was Jackson, assertive to the point of aggression one moment and unassuming the next.

Andy and Cody spoke for a few moments, throwing out things about the last year and how Garth had done things. The Knight men added their experience stating what they saw as potential.

Rafe shook his head. "I'm sorry to say it, but I really can't see myself working on this anymore past this week. I'm leaving soon. I prefer to just give it to a property manager and Andy. Let them figure it out." He looked apologetic but resolved.

The older Gentry siblings had similar olive coloring like their mother and dark hair and eyes like both parents. Piper had been different in some noticeable and unseen ways since she was born. She'd often wondered if she had been adopted because she had been the last and her coloring was so different. Blonde hair and the eyes of fog were not the standard family traits. Her mother had shown her photos of family members who looked like her. Nope, this was her family and she would stand up for what she thought they should do.

Rafe turned to Rosie. "What do you think?"

She stood and looked out the front room window. "I believe we should simply sell the ranch since no one really wanted it but dad. If we don't work it, then we shouldn't keep it. Besides, the profit that would come from the sale wouldn't be a bad thing. I think we will be throwing good money after bad if we try working it."

After her siblings had their say, they turned towards Piper with expectant looks on their faces. Piper looked at Jackson. He nodded.

"As you know, I'm pretty good at making things work. I have my own company that invests in properties and ventures of all kinds, turning them around and reselling them at a healthy margin of profit. I do a good amount of business in micro-investing suffering few losses. I have pulled the books, and I think I have a fair idea where things are now."

Piper looked over at Andy as he broke in. "I don't know if they're accurate. We did have several substantial losses this year."

She nodded. "Understood and there will need to be a formal review of the ranch. I have a good ranch property assessor I'm willing to bring into the mix to solidify our numbers."

"Piper, honey, I know it's hard but I think I've got a good handle on what we have and don't have," said Andy, a tinge of hurt feelings in his words.

"Yes, I know, but I think, with second opinion and a little investment, it's possible to turn things around. I can make that happen. It isn't that the ranch wasn't profitable, it simply seems like it was a lot of work for less profit than it should have had. That's why I'm the perfect choice for the ranch."

"What?" asked a surprised Rafe. "I thought you didn't care about the place. I mean, you live such a high and sophisticated life. Your hair is always done up, you're dressed to the nines, and you run in high circles now."

"Packaging, Rafe, all for show. Actually, to be honest, until I moved into that life I didn't realize I would miss the place as much as I do. When I come here I don't feel the need to dress the window if you will. Let me get my people to do some research on what makes these places profitable, and then I'll look at how at least one of those options might work here."

Rosie asked, "Would you really be able to make a profit? I mean, I know you have your own business and all but this is big."

Piper smiled at the sound of disbelief from her older sister. What her siblings didn't know about her would fill a library. Piper was the younger child by five years behind Rosie who was three years behind Rafe. That left Piper to grow up her last years without a sister on hand. Indeed, most of her growing up had been accomplished without sibling assistance.

"I really love this place, Rosie. I don't know animal husbandry or anything like that, but I can figure out what is needed and hire good people like Andy here for their expertise."

She loved the smell of the grass and the wildflowers, the buzz of the bees and the beauty of the butterflies. She enjoyed the tranquility of a stream in the immensity of pastureland.

Rafe was careful not to disregard his youngest sister's expertise. "Isn't your plate full now?"

"I'm looking at that too. You know, when I was at college," Piper continued, "I was taking international finance and economy with real world applications. It was stressful. So when I would get weekend breaks, I'd race home to the ranch to do nothing more than lie on the grass in the middle of the field with the blazing sun warming my face. I love this place."

It was her solace. She had her own special place at the stream and in the woodland that was on one side of her father's property and she wasn't ready to give that up.

Walker spoke up. "Yes, but you need to be realistic. You should look at the books and not romanticize this decision. I know your company is international now, but how many ranches have you invested in?"

"Good point. None to date, however I know how to make the money. Let me look at the books closely to see just how much profit dad made last year and how much we could make."

She knew that the ranch didn't have to make money, that it was all free and clear of liens. They could sell all the stock and just keep the property. However, she hoped that wouldn't be their ultimate course of action.

She looked pleadingly around the room after it erupted into differing points of view and what ifs. "I want it to make a profit not just sit here unused."

"I don't want to do anything, so if you can make a profit for us great, but if not, sell. That is my opinion, but I'll go with whatever you and Rafe agree on." Rosie walked back over to her seat and flopped in it.

Rosie, whose husband took control of all their finances and all their business transactions, was entirely happy to be done with her part of the decisions. The relief could be seen on her face and heard in her sigh.

Rafe was a little different. He cocked his head to the side and looked at Piper for a moment before shrugging his shoulders as if to say *do what you want.*

"Okay, wonder woman, if you want to pore over the books, figure it out in the next couple of days while Rosie and I settle other necessary business, that's not a problem." Rafe shook his head at his baby sister.

"Great," said Piper, "I'll know by the time you leave."

Piper looked over at Jackson when the others began chatting about different things. "You don't think I'm crazy, do you?"

"Nope, but I do want you to know that if you don't find that you want to make a go of it or feel it's not your ball of wax once things are laid out, I'm interested, so consider me before any other offers. I'd like to have you next door to me but if that isn't going to happen, let me be the one who gets first chance at giving you a fair price."

"Sure, but it won't happen."

"I hope not because I like the idea of having you around." He leaned over and brushed his lips lightly over hers but did not further engage. It was not enough and entirely too much contact with this potent man. He looked up. "Come on guys, time to hit the road. Morning comes awful early."

It was several days later as Jackson was sitting at the breakfast table after everyone had finished, that his ranch manager asked him what was going to happen with the property next door. Jackson leaned back a bit in his chair, turning sideways to look Cody fully in the eye.

"Well, I'm not really sure right now. Piper's still thinking she might want to take on the running of the ranch. She has it in her head that she can make the ranch more profitable than it was. She might be right. There did seem to be a lot of unused grazing land so it remains to be seen."

"Yeah, well I was talking to Andy yesterday afternoon, and he seems to think that the two older kids want to just sell and get rid of it. They told Piper again last night they just want to unload it. She pitched a fit and told them she would buy them out. She really wants to keep it. You weren't here often when Piper was a teenager, you were in college, but she did a lot of the running of that place when she was home before she graduated from high school. After she went to University of Texas, she never really came back around except the occasional weekend trip. I thought she'd pretty much outgrown the ranch. Sounds like I was wrong."

"What do you mean exactly? She was just a kid so how could she have pretty much run the place?" Jackson leaned in a little as he listened to Cody fill him in on how things were when Piper was home.

"Yeah, that's what I would've said if I hadn't been around when it was going on. You were gone so the day-to-day things happened over there without you seeing. Garth pretty much gave that girl free rein when she wanted to try a new direction with something on the ranch. It was the damnedest thing but she would research everything, make meticulous charts, lists, then she would organize everyone, and put it into action. I'll be darned if it didn't always work. Her dad said she was a genius and after seeing what she did especially those last two years of high school and what she's made of her company, I'm not arguing."

"Everyone has their limit though Cody. Piper is still young and has an incredibly intense corporation that she runs, hell, that she created. Working with the land is different. A ranch is different from finance. Yes, one works into the other but you gotta love the land. It must be part of who you are; as though some mornings if you didn't have it to touch, to be on, to walk it, to work, life just wouldn't be worth living."

"I get what you're saying Jackson, but you don't know this part of Piper like I do. You say the land has to be in you. I'm telling you, she communes with it and has an affinity not a lot of kids her age did. She put a lid on it so she could succeed in business but she loves this place. It'd be a shame if she couldn't try to make a go of it." Cody stood up pushing his chair back. Grabbing for his hat off the seat next to him, he prepared to leave but shared an intense stare with Jackson. "The man who gets that girl will have found a treasure. The problem will be learning to be a good steward of her riches. I'll see ya later."

Cody began to put his Stetson on as he walked to the door, letting the kitchen screen door lightly slam shut. Jackson watched Cody walk across the yard to his cabin and he wondered at the words Cody had said. He didn't disagree that Piper was a smart cookie but too much on your plate, hungry as you might be, would still be too much.

He stood a couple more minutes shifting his gaze out across the front yard and wondered how long before he could sink deep in her sweetness. Take his place in her life and bring her into his. It had been too long. Not that he hadn't embraced the softness of other women but considerably less than a man in his prime who didn't hold a place in his heart for another. It had been a lie he told himself, of course. Piper owned his very being.

He wondered if they'd survive a relationship where she belonged to him again, because he knew where his relationships typically went since being with Piper, nowhere. Oh, the women were willing, he just couldn't commit. No, he could wait a while and see what Garth's kids came up with on how to handle the ranch and if he needed to, he'd step in and help do a little guiding. That was if Piper would continue to allow it.

Chapter 3

The next day after she had made a call to her research department, which sounded big but consisted of two highly resourceful people, Piper asked Andy if he would go for a walk with her. She needed help to understand the daily operations.

Piper tried to step out of her emotions over the loss of her father, the enormity of the ranch workings, and step into her professional thought box. The hat fit but the shoes seemed immense. Her thoughts next went to Jackson. She relaxed in his mellow, deep voice, the sound of reason when she went her visions went a little wild.

Andy had been the ranch manager since Piper was a young girl, and he'd never left. Andy had signed on as a new hand soon after Piper was born, and she couldn't remember a time or day that if they needed him, Andy wasn't there. Piper had relied on him almost as much as she had her father when learning the ropes.

Between the two men, they taught her how to run a ranch. They taught her what was important and to love the land. She'd learned the land part, but wished she'd paid more attention to the *running the ranch* part. Oh, she had a few good ideas and her dad had let her run with them. They'd worked but she never knew if her dad and Andy didn't make it happen behind her back. It was that uncertainty that stalled her going ahead, firing with both barrels.

After spending a couple of hours with Andy, putting things in her mind as to what the research was saying and what the reality on the ranch was, she needed some thinking time. She trusted Andy but she wasn't seeing it the same as he did. They parted company for the evening with plans to meet up again the next morning, after chores had started. As Piper was walking, she remembered a grove of plum trees not very far from the fence line, and that's where she headed.

The intense heat eased as the sun lowered. July in Texas would never be cool, but evening brought sweet relief. She smiled at that because, while she was seen as the sophisticate outside of these borders, her siblings never understood why anyone would stay in the broiling heat purposely. Her grandmother had been the same way.

Her sister lived in a modern house. Tony made a good modern income, and they were happy. Rafe seem to be satisfied with his choices. He certainly lived all over the world all year long. Piper wondered if she was still content with her own life. Maybe content wasn't the word but satisfied. She lived in Austin, and it was a thriving city with every amenity known to man. Some were unknown to most men, but she loved it or at least she thought she did.

She knew she had a small company with a big footprint. She had begun to field several offers she considered lowball, but they were rising. Last week, she had one that was close to market value. Not that she would sell for anything close to that number, but she did wonder, if they hit the right number, would she pack it all in. Unlike a year ago, now she rather thought she would consider it. If she decided to take on this ranch's challenge, it might be her new proving ground.

She looked up and saw, running along the fence line in front of her, the prize she'd sought. Beautiful plums that made her mouth water lay before her. She couldn't believe how large they were. She pushed her hat back and looked down at her bare hands wishing she had remembered to grab some rawhide gloves. Never mind, she'd done this many times as a kid.

She thought about climbing the fence and then climbing up the tree, but she didn't want to risk staining her slacks and then chastised herself for coming out in slacks in the first place. She knew better than that, and she wouldn't make that mistake again. She calculated her best move to grab several plums she saw on one large branch hanging over the fence line. She eyeballed the fence putting her hands safely on the barbed wire. She grabbed the wooden post and took her first precarious step on the wire.

While she knew the wire would probably hold her without any problem, it jiggled and cost her a moment of reconsideration before it steadied. As its movements slowed, she got her balance again. Still holding the post, she took the next step onto the middle wire. It didn't rock as much as she figured it would. Good, her feet were stabilizing each other. Gaining courage, she took her lower foot and placed it up to the third and top wire. That's when it happened.

She was steady for a moment until she lifted her hands off the wooden posts and tried to balance herself by grabbing onto the branch. It seemed fine as there was little movement in the wire and she quickly reached up with her other hand to grab a plum right over her head. A squirrel chose that exact moment to run from the branch above her head towards the tree trunk chattering loudly.

Startled she pulled back quickly, too quickly. She was able to go into a full standing position, unsupported, for a split second. Almost immediately she was completely off balance and falling backward. Frantic, she attempted to make purchase on something, anything that would save her from the pain of contact. In the blink of an eye, her legs and feet twisted firmly in the barbed wire. She came down hard.

Piper saw the proverbial stars when her head hit the ground. It was more like black spots. The fall knocked the wind out of her causing her chest to hurt. She lay still for a few moments trying to get her bearings again. Unfortunately, her hat flew off when she fell. She lay in the beating sun, her head unprotected. It was brutal.

When she thought she had recovered enough, she tried to pull her legs out of the barbed wire, but they didn't easily release. She lay another minute and pulled again only to feel the same resistance as she had the first time. She thought to take her slacks off, but they were tangled in the barbs with not enough leeway to allow her to wiggle out of them.

Her head was beginning to ache, and trying to sit up again wasn't advised so she waited a few more moments getting up the courage to try a third time. In the moments that she was waiting, she coerced her fuzzy brain to calculate what she could do to get out of the fix she was in.

Thinking was increasing her nausea. As it calmed a little, she pulled out her cell phone. No service. Nothing had changed in that regard. There wasn't a tower. She'd offer a square of land to get a tower put in. This was ridiculous. She wanted to cry.

She had just about prepared herself for some substantial skin tearing when she saw someone coming up on the other side of the fence line. He was still a distance away, but she hoped whoever it was, would come close enough for her to call out. No matter how much it would hurt, she'd do her best to be loud.

After what seemed like an interminable amount of time, the man got closer and she could identify him. Piper suddenly didn't want to be caught all tangled up in the barbed wire like a city girl. It was true she had a lot to learn about the ranch that she didn't learn in her childhood, but that didn't mean that her ego was strong enough to weather getting caught tied up in barbed wire, and not feel the mortification of it.

She tried to take her boots off using the wire as leverage but unfortunately, these weren't work boots, these were fashion boots. They zipped, and were also known as "useless on a ranch" boots. She began to struggle in earnest trying to get out of the wire before the rancher came up on her. However, now he appeared to be approaching quickly. All she managed to do was rip her clothing and skin further as she increased her movements.

In her renewed efforts to release her feet from the entanglement, her pants' hem ripped loudly. She moaned.

Why didn't I just climb the stupid tree? I wouldn't be in this predicament. I wouldn't be stuck here like an idiot. I wouldn't be embarrassed, and I'd have my hat. My body wouldn't ache and I wouldn't feel sick. Now I have none of the things I wanted and all of the things I don't.

Giving up, Piper was resigned to her fate. She laid still until the man came within ten feet of her.

"Hey, baby cakes. You have yourself trussed up pretty well here. I'm not sure what you were planning to do, but I have a good idea this wasn't your goal."

That voice always did naughty things to her core and it was, somehow infuriating that he had such control over her libido.

"What an excellent deduction, Sherlock. Could you get me out of this mess?"

"I could if I thought you'd ask nicely. You're technically trespassing, you know. How about you try that again?"

"I fell on my property, so no, I'm not trespassing."

He was teasing but she wasn't in the mood. It was what he did when they were kids and he was trying to figure out how to get her out of one scrape or another.

"True enough. But that plum next to you was from the tree on my property. Got a little hungry I see." He kept talking as he walked around her lower half, looking at her predicament. "I think you understand that in a moment like this, an attitude of gratitude would go a long way." His words and tone were teasing and chastising at the same time.

"I must have knocked it over with my hand when I fell backwards from the overhang on *my* property. I was trying to grab anything that wasn't barbed. It seemed like a good idea."

"Mm hm." He waited.

"A gorgeous butterfly was on that tree trunk and I was just trying to get a closer look."

"Mm hm."

She thought he would ask something else, but he didn't. Piper had been looking at Jackson as he stood on the other side of the fence waiting for a polite request and it took a minute for her mind to process what he was asking her.

Once again, she realized how tall he was. From her vantage point, she could see that he, unlike her, had work boots and blue jeans on. Acceptable wear for daily ranch work.

Today, unlike at the memorial, his Stetson was a worn and obviously a much-loved companion that looked at home on his head. She could still see some curling dark hair coming out around his ears and he sported a gorgeous worker's tan that had been hidden in his long sleeves of the past few meetings. He was so damn handsome he took her breath away.

Jackson stepped close to the barbed divider and squatted down on his haunches to look into her eyes. He tipped his hat backwards so that it gave him more vision and it gave her full view of his face.

She put her hand up to shield the sun from her own eyes as he winked at her. She relaxed some. He glanced up at the sun. That's when she noticed the pounding in her head was worse. She tried to move again, and it caused her to moan in discomfort. That seemed to change his teasing, and he jumped into action. He scaled the fencing and walked to her head, reaching out for her hat.

"Sorry, Jackson, please help me out of this. I'm beginning to feel the effects of the fall and sun."

"Shit. I'm sorry baby. I got caught up in looking at you. You're so damn beautiful." He shook his head. "Okay sugar just lay there for a moment while I untangle your feet." He picked up her hat and put it over her head and forehead. She knew instant relief. "You had a nasty fall there. I'm sorry I was teasing you. It was mean of me. Tell me how you're feeling?" She peered up at him through the corner of her face he hadn't covered and saw him studying her intensely as he stood up. He didn't wait for her answer as he walked over towards her tangled feet.

"I think the worst thing hurt is my pride, but my head is pounding, and I think I must've scratched my legs on the barbed wire." She tried to get up, and he laid a calming hand on her calf. Funny that that is what energized her into reacting because she was used to being the one in control. She wasn't good at allowing anyone else to tell her what to do. Not even Jackson Knight.

"Hold on, baby, let me work on this and get you untangled so we can make sure you're really okay."

"I'm really okay, Jackson. I told you that I'm just stuck. It was stupid of me."

She was embarrassed, which fueled her temper. Add to that her pain level that was rising, her fuzzy head, her queasy belly, and she was walking on the edge of polite. She saw his eyebrow shoot straight up as though he couldn't believe that she was taking that tone with him.

The Jackson she used to know would have spanked her after an escapade like this one. Not upset she got tangled up but she'd done it so inappropriately dressed and he would have been right, she did know better.

He wouldn't have seen anything cute about the fall, her laying in the heat, or any of the other outcomes from climbing the fence. Her tummy had those pings she experienced whenever she thought of Jackson's situation fixers totally unrelated to the nausea from the heat and the fall. It was a love-hate relationship she had with those spankings, and right now she was experiencing both at the thought of his hand bouncing off her ass. Damn she was back to tingling.

But looking at him now, she doubted he was the same man today. He was gentle and passionate, not the same impatient, disciplining one she had experienced almost a decade ago. She realized that made her a little sad. She felt her feet loosen in their entanglement. In just a couple more minutes, her feet were gently laid to the ground.

"Hold on a minute, baby, I have to look at..."

She rolled over and waited a few seconds before scooting out from under the fencing. She rose to her knees and then scrambled to stand up when the world tilted. Before she knew it, he was next to her giving her a steady hand.

"Dammit Piper Kay, do you have no self-preservation? If I'd known..." He got quiet. When he next spoke, his low, dark voice sent shivers up her back.

"Baby cakes, how long have you been laying out here?"

She tried to shrug but it hurt. "A little while."

"We are going to discuss why you didn't lead with that little bit of information later. Right now, I want you to listen to me and go slow." She didn't want him to know how nauseous she was on top of being stupid. His voice was firm. She move jerkily. "Piper. I said to..."

She had to cut him off before she cried. "I'm fine I just need to stand here so I can get my bearings and things will be good." She vaguely heard her wobbly voice.

"I don't know about that," he said as he gave her his strength. His concern was heard loud and clear. He seemed hesitant like they hadn't spent any time together in nearly a decade. God she missed his bossy self.

She tried to stand upright again and stabilize. She lasted a few moments, then unconsciously grabbed his hand tightly as she tried to will the world around her to quit spinning. Just as she was about to take a step another wave of nausea overtook her, and she took short fast breaths to avoid vomiting. As she turned her head away from him, she promptly lost the battle.

"Nope that's enough. You sit down now. I don't want you going anywhere. Do you hear me? I don't want you getting up. I don't want you rolling over. Lean back against this post right here and get your bearings. Daddy is going to clip this wire, so I can get my horse over here. Then you're going to sit right in front of me so I can get you home. That knock on your head was harder than you thought, and the sun likely made it worse. We might even need to call the doctor."

"I said I'm okay."

He called himself Daddy, again. She hadn't heard him say that since referring to their dynamic in high school and college. Those kids seemed like a lifetime ago. It made her feel vulnerable. Why didn't that make her angry? No clue but it did leave her wanting.

Piper didn't sound okay. She sounded far away and ill even to her own ears. She panted and winced as she tried to gain her balance, but her breath continued to come a little faster than it should have, making it hard to hide her headache and the stinging from her legs. She felt the hot tears slide down her cheeks.

"I've seen this before and I'm not about to pretend you might not be hurt just because you want to act, not well I might add, that you aren't." Jackson didn't make a move but kept a close watch on her. "Tell Daddy how long have you really been out here, sugar?"

"A little bit. Look, I can scoot under the fencing, really."

She held the side of her head and tried to roll over to her knees one more time and Jackson squatted down in front of her, blocking any further movement. She could feel the strength in his grasp as he held onto both of her shoulders.

"If you move at all, I'm going to paddle your rear end so hard your ass will throb in time with your head. Do I make myself clear, Piper Kay?"

There was no denying the authority with which those words were spoken. As incensed as Piper normally would have been with that type of threat her head really did hurt. Besides, this Jackson she knew. This Jackson she fell in love with as a teenager.

"Daddy needs an answer baby."

"Yes sir," was her weak but totally natural response. There, he did it again. Should she protest? She should but later. Tomorrow. Or she could accept it.

"That's my sweet girl. I'm not being condescending; I'm fairly certain you have a concussion. Did you pass out?"

"No, but I know I was close," came her whispered words. "I'll repair the fence if you cut it."

"All right. You can do it with me, but not today. You're doing well. Just stay with me honey. Hold on a bit longer."

She preened in his praise and then rejected her weak response with a sound of disgust. It was all she could do. She waited for Jackson to take care of things, like he always did.

Chapter 4

Jackson patted her leg gently, rubbing it before he stood up. He walked his horse directly to the fence post dropping the reins over the barbed wire partition. He caught Piper watching him as he reached through the fence line into his saddle pack to pull out his gloves. He grabbed his wire cutters and neatly snipped the barrier. He mentally added fence repair to his long list of chores for that night or the next morning. When he compared that to his sweet bit of sugar on the ground, it didn't compare.

Walking his horse carefully through the gap left after he pulled away the wire, Jackson made eye contact with Piper as he created the pathway and winked. He performed some makeshift tying and twisting of wire, replacing the fencing the best he could before shoving the clippers and the gloves back in the saddle pouch. He pulled a fat yellow ribbon out of the pouch and tied it to the post, for locating it easier when coming back to fix it.

She must have felt somewhat better because when Jackson reached down to pick Piper up off the ground, she swatted at his hands. He answered her swat with a smack of his own on her thigh. She squealed and tried to scramble away but he held her steady and in place. After staring into his eyes and seeing the stern warning on his face, he was satisfied when she abandoned her efforts.

"Fine, I'm an ungrateful brat. I just want to go home." Piper said as she let him assist her onto his horse, without any more interference.

He said nothing but quickly swung up behind her, settling her right behind the horn and walked back towards the house. After a couple of moments he smiled as she rubbed her smacked thigh. His smile grew when she leaned back into his chest. He wrapped his left arm around her, happy she held onto it instead of the saddle. He could enjoy her soft lilac scented blonde hair and the easy trust they had, but not make her irritable with his satisfaction. Jackson didn't think she would like him relishing the fact that his attention-getter was still effective.

"Does it hurt much?" he asked gently as he leaned closer to her ear.

"What are you referring to, my feet, my legs, my head, my thigh or...?"

"All of it."

"Well, my head is pounding, my foot is swollen, I think my ass is bruised, and my thigh feels attacked. I can understand the rest, but one was not self-induced so funny enough, it hurts the worst."

"Sounds like another attack of pride. Need to get over that if you want to do well in ranching."

"Who says I've decided to take on the ranch?"

"You will. I was watching you just enjoy the land a while ago. You'll stay."

"You mean you watched me fall?"

"Nope, I watched you enjoy your walk and when I noticed you hadn't come back, I went to check things out. Good thing, too, because who knows how long you would have been there."

She was more subdued when she apologized. "I'm sorry for being so nasty. Thank you for coming to find me."

"You are Garth's daughter, for sure. He was one heck of a rancher and an incredible neighbor, but he couldn't play poker or chess worth a damn. I hope you've learned how since leaving home." Jackson chuckled, and Piper joined him only to moan her discomfort. Jackson kissed her head.

"You want me to play poker?"

"No, I like that you can't play poker, but chess would have been nice."

"I tried to teach Pops some strategies," laughed Piper delicately, then moaned at the pain. "Except he said it wouldn't be fun if he had to keep thinking about how to win. He just wanted to enjoy a game with his friends."

"We did have laughs over his moves, but the challenge was better in checkers. He was such an open book, poker was just wrong to play with him. So, baby, how does your Gentry World Investments do these days?"

He wanted to get her home faster but that would have made her feel worse, so he settled for kissing her pounding head.

"Good."

"It was a while before I knew that your family owned that company. Garth never said anything at all. I mean, he said you were in the world of finance but that was it. It took some research to find you in the early days, but then your company hit the stock exchange and that was it. Now you're everywhere."

She leaned her head back on his chest. "I own GWI. It isn't a family business. Most people don't know what that stands for and my advisors said the abbreviations were better for business, but it started as Gentry World Investments. Really that's all my dad ever got of the company was that it's high finance, as he called it and said so long as I was happy so was he." She paused. "Did you really research me?"

"Yes, I really researched you. I couldn't let you do something else with your life without me and not know what that was. You've created a successful business at a young age."

"Thanks, that means a lot to me. Do you think you could explain that to my siblings? I am just goofing around with play money to them. And I didn't do it without you purposely. I just needed to spread my wings away from here. But now, with the ranch to figure out, I'm a little out of my element. I'm not sure what to do exactly. I'm going to look at the books again later."

"Tomorrow. Today, you are taking it easy because while I think you should get checked out, I won't force it if you do as I say when we get you inside."

She ignored him and continued on. "I still don't have the whole picture on how things were run Jackson, and I don't have much time before I must make the decision."

"Well, I'm sure you can do it if anyone can. Here, we are at the back door. Now Piper, do not try to get down off the horse yourself. You let me help you or I will put a matching smack on your other side, got me?"

"Yes," she answered with the tiniest bit of a pout.

Jackson smothered his smile. This woman was still some kind of nice and no matter what she did with her day he wanted her curled up with him at night. He'd decided at the funeral service that he was going to play his cards right with her this time. She was never going to leave him again, and he was more determined than ever after today. He carefully hauled her off his gelding, gently standing her on the ground as he allowed his horse to graze on the grass off the back porch.

Jackson walked with her to the couch, got her some cold water and frozen peas for the back of her head. As he started to leave to tell Rosie to come and watch her for a while, Andy walked into the room. After prying the story out of Jackson, he turned back to Piper, and asked her the question Jackson was sure he had the answer to.

"What were you doing on the fence anyway?"

Piper had the dignity to blush, "I was getting something."

"What could have been so damn important that you had to risk your safety by climbing over rather than through the fence?"

"Plums." Piper ducked her head as she said it, her blush rising and deepening.

"Plums?" Andy shook his head.

Jackson followed through. It was as he had suspected. "You risked your safety for plums? That's as bad as your butterfly story. I should've spanked your ass. Don't you do that again, hear me. If you want plums, I'll get you plums, safely."

"I'll get my own plums thank you. I just saw them and wanted them like when I was a kid. I won't make the same mistake twice." Piper's embarrassment fueled her irritation. "I know I shouldn't have tried to stand on the fence. Normally I'm on a horse and just reach up but..." she shrugged. "I didn't want to mess up my slacks by climbing the tree."

"I see how that worked out for you. You'd think my super intelligent woman should have known not to try to climb the barbed wire." Jackson gave her a censuring look.

"All right already, I know I screwed up. I won't make that mistake again. Can we drop it?" She reached her hand up to hold her head.

Jackson was instantly contrite. "Okay, baby cakes, you need to calm down for now and let Rafe and Rosie take care of you." He turned to Andy. "I think she has a concussion, at least."

"A mild one." Her look was the old stubborn Piper.

"She didn't pass out, but she did puke once. So we need to watch her. Piper, if you take this ranch on, you're going to have to think before you act. In fact, you need to learn to think differently. The elements will kill you and so will plenty of other things if you don't keep your head in the game." He leaned down and kissed her cheek. "I have waited too long for you to come home to have to worry about your safety and losing you." Just as he was finishing his speech and was standing to turn around, Rosie came into the room and jumped into the conversation.

"Well, hello gorgeous." She was looking at Jackson. Ever since Rosie was absolved of any big responsibilities on the ranch, everyone noticed she had relaxed considerably. "Is this what took you so long, Piper? If Jackson is the reason, I forgive you." She looked over at her sister for the first time and whistled. "Wow, like it rough, huh, sis? Better not let Rafe see you. He is in the protective stance these days. I think Jackson brings it out in him."

"No and shut up. Have you been in the cooking sherry because you are amazingly lacking in the filtering department today, Rosie. You would think living in Europe would have tempered your tongue, but I guess even the Vatican couldn't do that. And what would Tony say?" Piper gingerly leaned her head back on the sofa.

Jackson handed her several painkillers and water.

Rosie had the decency to blush. "Sorry, not sure where that came from," she said leaving the room without asking about Piper.

Jackson wasn't about to allow Piper to ignore her symptoms of concussion, maybe dehydration and possible heat exhaustion. He also wasn't going to let Rosie ignore them either. He knew some things about his girl that Piper would not have wanted her family to know. He had his contacts in Austin, one was a good friend from college who did background checks and other things. He asked him to check up on her and what came back was she was a go-getter and worked late many nights. She went home alone almost every day, even Sunday because she chose to live her life alone. That wouldn't fly any longer.

Jackson walked into the kitchen behind Rosie. "Rosie, Piper needs to clean those cuts from the barbed wire, take more aspirin in four hours, and drink some water. Maybe take a nap as well and definitely not go out in the sun the rest of the day."

"Jackson, the only way I'll be able to get that to happen is if you handle it. Rafe went into town to see about paperwork and Piper hasn't listened to me in fifteen years."

"Are you kidding me? You're older than she is."

Rosie shook her head. "I'm sure I don't have to remind you how bull headed she can be when she's made up her mind."

"That stops now." He walked into the living room and found it empty.

Rosie followed him. "She must have gone into her room."

"Alone. Stubborn woman. Okay, lead the way."

Rosie pointed to the bedroom that had always been Piper's and stepped back as the big man took the length of the hall in four long strides. Jackson opened the door and Piper groaned when she saw him.

"Jackson, please, I don't feel well."

"I know, baby, I just need to make sure you're taking care of yourself. Where is your aspirin?" She pointed to her little bathroom.

Jackson walked in the bathroom and rummaged around for a few minutes before he came back out with assorted supplies in his hand. He placed the pain reliever on her side table and set the refilled water glass down next to it as well.

"I can do it myself, thank you."

"Drink it. All." He waited. "Now, Piper."

She did but grunted and turned her body slightly away from him. He laid the supplies on the bed and then patted her hip.

"Sweetheart, let me take care of you. Your head hurts and your legs are scratched up. You're dehydrated, and I need to make sure you're okay before I go home."

She shook her head carefully and said, "Please let me do it. Or Rosie could help."

"Rosie said you wouldn't let her if she tried."

"Tattletale," she murmured.

Jackson could hear the sound of capitulation in her voice and pushed firmer.

"Piper, take your pants off."

The look of alarm almost made him laugh. "I'm not going to take advantage of you. I'm going to take care of you." He wiggled his eyebrows. "That is, unless you want me to do both."

Her look held disbelief. His held his merriment. She smiled slightly.

"I've heard that before, Jackson Knight."

He loved hearing her use his name but he'd prefer Daddy in private. "Okay, enough now. I'm not going to make love to you when you're hurt and need rest. I want you to be fully engaged when I take you."

"Oh, you plan to do that at some point do you?"

"Yes, ma'am, I definitely do." He nodded at her torn slacks. "Now, take them off or I'll do it for you. If I do it, I will take care of your backside first before I take care of your cuts."

"If I am too hurt for sex, Jackson, you can believe I am too hurt for your brand of machismo."

"Right."

He reached for her pants. Piper whimpered and then made a sound of impatience but tried to sit up. Jackson stood back with his arms folded as she swung her legs over the side of the bed. She reached down to remove her destroyed slacks causing her to inhale sharply.

"Sit back baby. I'll take them off, no penalty. Your tongue makes me respond as I did when we were kids. I need to stop that and you need to stop acting the brat at every turn. Let Daddy take care of you."

She nodded her head slightly in agreement. "Jackson, I'm not sure... I mean... the daddy bit."

He started to work on her slacks carefully so he didn't cause her any further distress. "We can work on that. I thought you wanted a daddy in your life."

"Not a daddy, I wanted you however you came. I'm just not sure I can give over to you when you want anymore. I'm different now."

"I am too. The relationship will morph into what we are looking for; what we are missing in our lives. I love it when you call me Daddy, but I've lived fine with Jackson my whole life. It isn't what you call me it's how you see me. It's how we are together, that matters."

"Okay." She sighed. "Slacks, what was I thinking? I won't make that mistake again." She hissed when she sat up straighter. "No more horseback riding until I get better acclimated, either. I haven't done much this last week, but I have been feeling every bit of it."

"You need to do it a little every day, extending it slow and steady. You'll be there again soon. Now let me lay you back so I can get to you better."

Piper opened her mouth. Jackson shook his head firmly. "Uh, uh, do not complain to me about anything. Behave and let me help you."

She wrinkled her nose and puckered her lips but didn't speak, just huffed her displeasure at being ordered about. She carefully slid back further on the bed with Jackson guiding her. She moved faster than he was guiding and hissed. She brought her legs up, feet flat on the bed, crossing her arms over her shirt covered breasts and sucked air in quickly.

"Hurts, huh? I told you to let me do this but you're one ornery woman. See what your stubbornness and irritation does? It hurts you more. Stop being so naughty and let me take care of you. I promise to be gentle, baby."

"How do you do this to me? I'm a grown woman with employees, a master's degree, a successful company and you treat me like a wayward child?"

"It's because you act like a wayward child sometimes. Now carefully scoot over."

She did, and he ignored her irritated body language and cleaned her legs with alcohol pads.

"Ow, ow, ow," she screeched.

"Sorry honey, I have to make sure they're clean to avoid infection."

"I think you're taking perverse pleasure from my pain."

"Nope," he said as he rubbed triple antibiotic cream on the scratches. Next, he used small bandages for the couple that looked deep. He patted her thigh.

"Okay baby cakes, roll over."

She did with less demonstrated attitude this time. "Don't spank me, Jackson. I can't believe you still think spanking is okay," she mumbled into the bed covers.

"I guess I never thought you would expect that I didn't. It's who I am. You've always known that." He continued to clean and bandage her scratches.

"I guess I thought you wouldn't do it any longer. I mean, we're adults."

He laughed. "I did think you would need less of them by now, but I'm not sure that's the truth of it." He put the first aid things away and returned to squeeze her bottom cheeks+. "Besides, you have such an alluring bottom. Maybe after we're settled back into a relationship, you won't need many. That's my theory, anyway." He rubbed her back gently to help release the tension he could see and feel.

"You're so pushy. Mmm, maybe, oh that feels so good."

"Piper?"

"Yeah?" she said with a sigh.

"I want to be clear. I want us to be together again. Try our relationship again."

"I know, I heard you. I haven't had my back massaged in ages. This is incredible."

"Glad you enjoy it. I love doing it. Pips?"

"Hmm?" she sounded drowsy. Good.

"If we start a relationship, you have to know up front that I love you."

"What? You can't know that, I mean it isn't logical. Oh, Jackson, that spot right there."

"Yes, I know," he put his heel in the place she indicated and smiled as she sighed. "I expect both of us to do our best to make this a permanent thing. I'm not playing games and I'm too old to want cock teasing."

"I was never a cock teaser." She tried to push up but he held her down with his hand.

"Uh, huh. What do you call dating hot and heavy until you go to college and one day, right after graduation, just not coming home? Never answering my calls or texts again?"

"Scared that if I did, I would be stuck on the ranch and never get to spread my wings to see what I could do. That's what I would call it because that's what it was."

"Honey, I would never keep you from doing what you want to do."

"So, I can put sheep in and some exotics?"

"What? No, you cannot put in sheep."

"Jackson?"

"Yeah," he said as he covered her up with a sheet.

"I've loved you to some degree half my life. I think that's why I never had a serious boyfriend. Well, that and the fact that I've lived for work since I started working. I'm willing to go in that direction if you are, but you have to know that I don't have much free time. I can delegate more but now with the ranch I might have even less time than I ever did.

"Even though you have been the subject of many a dream over the years, I've needed to focus to succeed in what is still very much a man's profession. Since I've been back this time, I have had sexy dreams almost nightly. But please, let's go slow. I need to go slow."

He kissed her cheek and the top of her head. His hand smoothed the dirty strands. "We have a good starting point to figure this thing out. But you need to rest. Rosie will check on you every hour to make sure you're okay." He hardened his tone. "And you will let her or when you are feeling better, I'm spanking that delectable ass."

"Fine, I'll let her."

He did his best to hide his amusement but wasn't completely successful. "Good girl, but you need to know that while I can be gentle and nurturing now, I'm also even more demanding than I was as a kid. I know what I want and that is you. That means I take a personal interest in your safety and welfare. It also means I don't want you to get into anymore jams without a cell. Better yet, a cell and a partner." He leaned in and kissed her neck. "In case you were wondering, that isn't a request."

Jackson realized he sounded dictatorial, and he'd have to work on his presentation with her, but she could've sustained a greater injury out there without a way to get help if he hadn't come along today. The thought wasn't worth developing. She hadn't and for that he was thankful.

"But there isn't a tower that reaches in that area of the ranch. And I don't need bossy to understand the value in things." She giggled a little from his kiss on her neck.

"At all? Maybe we need to look and see if it will connect to the local service. If not, you'll need one that works for the ranch. Cody and the guys all have one too. Mine makes it possible to call from most places on the ranch." He leaned in and kissed the crook of her neck under her ear.

"Got it, that tickles, Jackson." She lifted the shoulder below his lips.

Piper tried to roll over.

"No, I'm going to leave you to sleep. If I stay any longer, we'll be doing what you aren't ready to do."

"I could be."

"But not now." He leaned in and kissed her cheek. "Later, baby cakes." He gently patted her backside as he stood.

"Mmm, okay. I guess you're right." She ended her agreement with a yawn.

Jackson smiled at the little snore he heard before he reached the staircase. When he reached his hand out to push through the kitchen door he got Rosie's attention.

"I have to go, and Piper is sleeping. She promises to let you nurse her."

"I'm not that great at it but if she lets me, I can check every half hour to make sure she is moving around."

"Good. I'll be back later to check on her. I think she's fine but I'm just going to be cautious. Call if she gets worse."

"I don't know why she ever let you slip through her fingers."

"I understand why, but if things go the way I hope, she won't do it again. Besides, isn't the second chance at love supposed to be sweeter?"

Chapter 5

At five the next afternoon, Rafe fired up the grill for the beef flank and Clearwater catfish. Only place near that had that quality of catfish. Piper set her work aside to start making the vegetables and rice pilaf to go with the yeast dinner rolls she had rising in preparation for baking. Her dessert was simple, peach and pear cobbler with plum sauce.

Jackson and Cody showed up right on time. Rosie answered the door and ushered them into the living room, explaining that Piper was finishing her preparations and Rafe was outside manning the grill. The men decided that they would go out and keep Rafe company just as Andy arrived with Walker on his heels. Rosie poked her head out and asked the men on the deck what they wanted to drink.

"Where's Sawyer?" she asked Walker.

"Date," said Walker. Rosie lifted her eyebrow. "A cute little thing too young for him but old enough to understand he's a player." She nodded and disappeared in the kitchen.

Rosie returned with the requested beverages and handed Rafe his iced tea without fanfare when the other gentlemen grabbed their beers. It was a family understanding that due to Rafe's earlier difficulties in controlling his alcohol consumption he always, without comment, went for nonalcoholic beverages. If anyone noticed no one mentioned it.

The girls brought out the side dishes, while Rafe filled everyone's plate with their chosen entrée, leaving the extras in the middle of the table. The weather wasn't too hot. There was a warm evening breeze blowing, making it pleasurable sitting outside underneath the protective awning. Piper had let people sit wherever it was they were comfortable, and the seat left open for her was the one across from Jackson. Piper knew that her sister had orchestrated it that way.

Most people might've thought the seat next to someone you were interested in would be the prize seat, but Rosie thought the one across from them was the best seat. They could observe the reactions to things discussed and scrutinize each other's mannerisms. You could catch a lot of things and learn a plethora of noteworthy details if you are across from someone, rather than next to them.

Piper had learned that little trick from her sister and had used it in her business to gain important insights into future employees, future business acquaintances, and professional dealings. While Rosie always said Piper was the business savvy one, Piper always said if Rosie ever wanted a job in personnel she would have it.

Andy asked, "Rafe you said you have a new assignment, where's it going to be?"

"Funny you should ask that because I just got a call yesterday on that very subject. It seems there's trouble heating up in Fiji and while it's something that's been going on for a while, civil strife, there are some other fascinating side stories. Some things that might not be quite right from outside sources might be worth exploring. So they asked me to go and see what I can turn up."

"Dig up you mean," amended Piper. "I don't even know how you figure some of those tangled messes out, but you sure do. I could use a situation man in my foreign affairs office. So Rafe any time..."

"Yeah, that's something I might like to do but I'm not going to work for my sister. Sorry Hon." Everyone laughed and not one of the men misunderstood. A man just didn't work for his sister, or his mother, unless it was the family business. A baby sister who started her own corporation after graduating college did not qualify as family business.

"Well, you know where to go if you have need of a paycheck."

"Sorry sis, I won't ever need a paycheck that badly." The guys laughed. The girls just shook their heads.

The conversation went on that way, back-and-forth bantering, talking about everything under the sun except the ranch. There seemed to be an unspoken understanding that if the ranch were brought up, it would be by one of the three siblings. Piper had decided they wouldn't open the subject until after dinner, and they had gone back into the house to settle in comfortably.

When it looked as though everyone had eaten their fill, Rosie and Piper popped up to clear the plates and take care of the cleanup quickly, while the men took care of the grill and went inside to settle in, refreshing their drinks as they did.

When the kitchen was clean the girls brought in the cobbler topped with ice cream and coffee. After serving everyone a plate, Piper went around and offered plum sauce to go on top of the cobbler and ice cream.

That's when the conversation changed.

Everyone was complimenting Piper for her dessert and all of them for the meal when Cody asked what the sauce was made from.

"Plum, the sauce is made from plums," answered Piper, happy she had made the dessert before she went on her ride yesterday.

Jackson cut his eyes in the direction of Piper, sat his bowl down, and said in a quiet voice, "Did you go back and get the plums, Piper?"

"What do you mean, did I go back and get them? I made the sauce if that's what you're asking."

Rosie felt the tension roll off Jackson but couldn't understand where it came from. To try and defuse the stiffness, she said, "Piper is actually a good cook she just doesn't have anyone to cook for, so we were really lucky she wanted to cook the sides for us tonight. I was getting a little tired of microwavable things."

"Yes, ma'am a really good cook," said Jackson. "I'm just concerned where the plums came from and how she got them. A day ago she didn't have a lot of luck getting them, and she and I have an agreement."

"I'm not sure what agreement you're talking about," responded Piper, "but I didn't sign any papers. And besides, it doesn't really matter how I got them. There was no mishap and we have plum sauce."

Piper turned to respond to a conversation that Rafe had opened up with Andy and Cody about the usability of the ranch, thereby effectively cutting off anything that Jackson would've said in response to her.

"So that's a good question," said Rafe, "How much would it actually cost to run the ranch as it is? I mean, what's the bottom line?"

"Well," started Andy, "I didn't do the books mind you, but I have a pretty good feeling that we were running a little close to the line during the winter these last couple years. Mostly because of the drought and it was expensive to keep your cattle. So we sold probably half the herd the last two years, just so we could afford to feed the other half and not go into the red. In fact, this last summer was the first time in about three years that we brought on new hands because the rains have been so good and the grass has been plentiful. We were able to restock a little bit before we lost Garth."

"And Andy, why didn't Pops just call me?" asked Piper.

"Don't take this wrong, but what was he going to call you about? That man had been running this ranch for close to forty years. There wasn't anything that he didn't already know about doing that you could have added to. And what you know is only what he taught you."

"Funds, I could have floated him and given him some great strategies on how to make the ranch more profitable during seasons of drought. I helped plenty of people get through the dry spells these last four years, but my own father doesn't ask me, so I guess I do take it a little personally. I helped others even though that's not my field of expertise."

Piper set her bowl down and stood up to walk into the kitchen to pull her emotions together. She didn't realize how hurt she actually was until she was sitting there talking about it after having buried her father. Someone walked into the kitchen behind her, and without looking she spoke thinking it was her sister or brother.

"I'm fine. I guess I didn't realize how much it hurt me that he didn't call me. I mean, he was Pops. Why wouldn't he call me for help?"

"Because he was your father," said the deep voice softly spoken.

Piper was startled it was Jackson who had come after her. Not one of her siblings and yet, she fully expected that he would have come after her. That was who this man was, a daddy through and through. The way he answered her touched something inside, and the tears began to stream down her face unchecked.

Piper was usually a master at controlling her emotions, both inwardly and outwardly. But there was no stemming these tears. She leaned over the sink, planting her elbows on the counter and putting her face in her hands as the torrent of tears overtook her.

She felt powerful arms come up to her shoulders, turn her around, and bring her into his chest. If she weren't so overwrought, she might've pushed him away. Instead, she grabbed his shirt with both hands and just cried while he held her gently and securely to him.

They stood there, Jackson speaking softly just above her ear while he smoothed her hair. He stood as though he had nothing else to do but hold her while she cried out all the avoided sentiment of the last week.

Tears never bothered Jackson. He wasn't like his father who never seemed to know what to do with tears. In fact, it frustrated his dad almost to the point of anger because he didn't know what to do when Jackson's mother would cry. She'd learned early that her husband, wonderful man though he was, could not deal with her heartbreaks and she found other ways to meet her emotional release.

Jackson's father was not a spanker like he and his brothers Sawyer and Walker. He wasn't a disciplinarian of much value to his kids or himself. He was a good rancher, but he dabbled in excesses and it was those excesses that brought Jackson's mother to tears most often.

Jackson had decided long ago that he would not run his relationships, or his house that way. He was a man of his word. He invested a lot of time in showing his integrity and he worked hard on what was now his ranch. Some people thought he took a hard line on too many things, but Jackson did not want to have to wonder if someone was dealing straight with him.

He had decided long ago that his wife and his kids would never doubt how devoted he was to them and how strong his love was for them. He concluded that the way to accomplish that was to instill the one thing that was missing in his father's relationship with him and that was discipline. Jackson absolutely believed that a disciplined life gave security because he had lived with the insecurity of not having it as a kid.

He also knew that for those who were brought up with love, security, and discipline there was a sense of belonging and, in a way, mutual ownership. It was a hard concept especially in a relationship. He tried to explain it once to a girlfriend, and she just thought he was bossy. After a few more disastrous responses, he decided that explaining it never really worked.

The best way was to let the woman see the result of his protection, his watchful care over her, and how he cherished them seemed to go over better. He actually had a few girlfriends who were okay with the daddy side and even the domestic discipline part occasionally. But for him it was an everyday, all-day way of life. Not a once in a while game to be indulged in the bedroom only. This was no game to him and the woman he ultimately married wouldn't see it as a game either.

Standing there holding Piper in his arms as she cried brought up all those protective instincts in him. It seemed so natural to hold her as she released her pain, and to soothe her as she tried to gain control of her tears. He rubbed his hands up and down her shoulders and arms trying to bring some tangible anchor that she could hold onto as he could feel her control increasing without causing her embarrassment.

FINALLY, SHE WAS ABLE to stand back from Jackson. She let out a self-conscious laugh at the predicament she was in, and it was obvious she was discomfited that he had witnessed it. But on the other hand, she felt a warm security, like a soft fluffy blanket, when his arms were around her and he was comforting her. Maybe a little embarrassment was worth the soothing.

It's not that she could remember anything he said even if she had been able to hear him over her heartbreak. Now that she thought about it, it seemed odd that no one else had come in, at least Rosie, to check on her. Did they simply allow Jackson to take care of it? The mortification was complete with that realization. She stood back and wiped her hands on her jeans as she groped for something to say to excuse her behavior away.

"I'm sorry. It isn't like me to lose control, normally. I don't know what happened or what came over me. I've cried all over your shirt. It's soaked. I bet you didn't think you'd come over here and hold a sobbing woman until her sanity returned. Some big CEO I am, I don't even seem to be able to regulate my emotions these days." She finished that sentence with a hiccup and quickly turned away from him.

"Stop, Pips. I'd hold you for hours if I thought I was giving you something you needed."

The water came on, falling into the sink as Piper interrupted its flow to splash water on her face. As she groped around for a towel, she had one placed in her hand and she patted her skin. She noticed Jackson hadn't said another word. He just stood there with one hand still on her arm, as though he was grounding her and keeping her secure.

This, among other things, was what she felt she'd been missing in her other relationships. Well, not that she had a relationship with Jackson now or that she should enter into one now. He wanted it, but he wanted it all and she had come to the sad conclusion that she wasn't the marrying kind. Better he find someone else.

But he said he loved you. He couldn't know that. It had been too long. She was too intense, too needy, and she knew it. It was just that it would've been nice to have this in her past relationships. The ones that didn't require her to live so far from her business and connections. And that spanked or daddied her.

Her brain was so scrambled she needed to get this evening over with, get some good sleep, and pull it back together. Unfortunately, they'd not even talked about the ranch really and she needed to get that done as well. She turned around from the sink, her resolve strong.

After looking up at Jackson she dropped her eyes to the floor. "Good, I'm good. What I worry about is that concern over the drought brought on undue stress for Pops, and maybe he couldn't handle it. But he didn't have a heart attack or stroke, did he, so I'm sure I am off the mark."

Jackson reached over and put his index finger under her chin bringing her face up, so he could look into her eyes. He thought she must've been the prettiest crier he'd ever seen. He could feel his cock give a little jump, and mentally told him to lay back down this wasn't the time. He sure hoped there would be a time soon because this little lady was someone he was interested in spending the rest of his life with. Strike that, would spend his life with.

"No sweetheart, it was not the reason Garth died and you know that. Now, are you sure you're ready to go back in there?"

His expression was as serious as his inquiry and Piper knew that she needed to be honest, because she felt he would see through anything less than sincerity.

"Well, not totally okay but okay enough. Thanks."

Piper gave him a little smile when he patted her arm.

"All right then let's go back and see what we can do about this ranch."

He pulled her to his side, wrapped his arm around her other shoulder, and started walking casually back into the family room. As they walked he asked her a few questions about her thoughts on the ranch until they came up on the rest of them. She sat in the chair she'd vacated earlier. He returned to his seat.

To the group's credit they simply turned and added them to the conversation they were already in, which was what kind of beef cattle had the best return these days. Piper sat for a few minutes talking and listen to their arguments in their reasoning behind running beef cattle before she added to the conversation.

"So I think we should run the bison as well as the Hereford we already have. I'd like to add some red Angus to the black and maybe add a Charolaise bull." The silence fell like a thick blanket on everything and everyone. Cody looked over at Piper and started to speak at the same time that Andy did.

"No way," said Andy.

"Why not?"

"Because we're just a cattle ranch, that's why. You're a cattle ranch." He spoke as though he were educating a small child who had never been privy to the concept of cattle.

"Says who? Bison bring good profits. I could have said sheep," said Piper.

Rafe sat back in his chair just as Rosie settled into hers. She seemed to be getting ready to enjoy the battle she knew was coming. Jackson also sat back in his seat on the sofa, leaned on the overstuffed arm next to him, and crossed one leg over the other as though he were waiting to see what else Piper had to say.

And he stimulated that further disclosure by encouraging her. "Go on."

Piper looked around and saw the different reactions in the room. Just as she would when she was trying to push a concept through to an investor, she settled in her seat more comfortably and reached down to grab her papers that she had put projections on ready to do battle.

"Okay so I've been doing some projections, some research, and I had one of my research assistants digging. These are the numbers and my reasons why I think adding bison and some cattle breed changes are a better way to go." Piper proceeded to lay out her plan.

Chapter 6

By the end of the evening everyone had worn out their reasoning and arguments and it was obvious that the room was divided into three schools of thought. The first line of thought was Piper's notion of exploring bison as the new back-up livestock. Cody and Andy, of course, knew cows. They knew beef, and they didn't think a ranch should run anything else, at least not the ranch they were on. Jackson, Walker, and Rafe were leaning towards Andy and Cody but they hadn't been absolute. Jackson was more certain. And Rosie had encouraged everyone's conversation for her own enjoyment.

It was getting late, so it was time to end the evening. As the guys were proceeding to the door Cody turned around and asked if she had any plum sauce left. He said he wanted to give it to his girlfriend to see if she could reproduce it because she was pretty good at that.

"Sure, let me go get it for you," answered Piper.

As she walked into the kitchen, Piper realized someone had followed her. She heard that same deep quiet voice, only with a little more authority. Now the man behind that voice asked her again where she got the plums. Piper knew what he was really asking but she thought she'd play with him for a bit, so she answered him in a roundabout way.

"The plums came from plum trees off the property, mine and yours I'm sure, so if you want me to replace however many plums I think came off your trees, I can. Although you have to understand it's going to be a guess." And she turned away from him so that he would not be able to see her smile.

"It sounds to me like someone wants a hot bottom pretty badly. I told you not to climb up there to get those plums, and it sounds like you didn't listen to me. I don't take kindly to be-ing ignored or disobeyed."

He had stepped up behind her, leaning down to speak into her ear, as she was pouring the sauce into a canning jar. She shrugged her shoulders nonchalantly as though it didn't real-ly matter, but the moisture in her lady bits told her something mattered.

She hadn't been turned on this intensely in a long time. This man was honey glazed, sex on a stick. It was a good feeling, helping to verify that she was still ignitable. She'd had more weeping anatomy in the last week than she'd had since leaving home.

"Sweetheart, are you listening to me? A man doesn't like to talk and not be heard."

"I heard you."

"That's not what I asked. I asked if you listen to me."

"Yes, I listen to you. I listened to you tell me that you didn't want me to get the plums without using something safe to stand up on."

"And so did you?"

He was still very close to her. So, close she could feel his warm breath and his hands on her hips and it took everything in her to not to lean back into that strength and comfort. But she didn't.

"Well, I did grab the plums, and I did sort of climb to get them, but I promise I did listen to you when you said I needed to stand on something safe."

"Let me get this straight. You did listen to me, but you still climbed to get the plums, which isn't minding to me."

"Well not exactly. See, I did climb to get the plums and I guess technically I didn't use something to support me that was overly sturdy. But I didn't get them from the tree, I got them from the cellar shelf so I guess I did mind you, sort of."

She screwed the top onto the jar and turned around to face his chest. He smelled good, like soap and fresh air and warm Jackson. Pulling herself away from the sweetness that was Jackson's arms she walked past him to deliver the plum sauce when she felt a swat on her butt. Not a hard one but one that was meant to get her attention, and it did.

"What the hell?"

"Uh, uh, ladies do not swear."

"That's ridiculous, of course they do. Ladies do just about everything and they are still ladies. Tell me why your hand met my butt, and the answer better be good."

"Just consider it the brat corrector. You were being a brat, and I was correcting your behavior. It's a simple concept."

"Well just don't let it happen again, because the bottom line is that I don't allow the assault of my person in any way. Ever." Her frown turned to a sugary smile that was met with a knowing one from Jackson.

"No baby cakes, the bottom line is that your bottom crossed the line, and it got put back where it belonged, toeing the line." He dropped a kiss on her lips, grabbed his Stetson and walked outside.

Sleep didn't come easily for Piper later that night and she hoped it didn't for Jackson, either.

THE DAY HAD BEEN LONG and hard. Piper had gotten up before the sun and driven into Austin to do some work, connect with her people in person and she had set up a luncheon for strategy talking with livestock experts. So, while she had actually thought she would try to add sheep on the ranch as well, they were probably out of the question due to many things, including market and prejudices in cattle country.

There were exotic livestock gaining in popularity but the experts still said what her men had said, "Run cattle."

They did agree that bison was on the rise and had a bright future in production markets. The overall difference was that she could run the operation smarter and make a better profit. After listening to their recommendations and making notes about where she could get better stock and recording the phone number of each person at the table, she returned to the ranch with a different mindset.

Sliding in under the line to eat with her family, Piper watched as Rosie put the finishing touches on dinner. It reminded Piper that she had never learned to cook entrees well. Oh, she could create lots of side dishes, and could do a mean hamburger and no one dared top her nacho supreme, but a corn soufflé like the other night? Nope, not even close. It hadn't mattered in her world before this but somehow, here on the ranch, it mattered. Again, not corn soufflés but ranch worthy meals.

She needed to pay attention to what Jackson liked to eat and make sure she could cook that at least. Or knew where to buy it, compromised her urban brain. But that took time and effort away from other things that were demanding those very things from her right now. Relationships took nurturing, and that is why she couldn't get involved with Jackson again. He deserved someone who was focused on him. She was focused on contracts, investments, and cattle.

That's what she was dealing with here, her urban and country brain. They started out the same and then quickly morphed into different ideas, methods, and even ethics. It was those same differences that were making it difficult to submit to Jack's ideals, such as discipline.

Oh, long before she was exposed to the world, Jackson was all she knew but now it wasn't that way. She had been to every continent and introduced to a variety of ways to enjoy a man. But Jackson wasn't just any man. He was bigger than life. More man than she could handle right now, maybe ever.

Piper smiled. Kink is not a word she would have ever connected with her down to earth cowboy, but it is what he had, a thing for spanking that matched his thing for daddying. He didn't call it anything and didn't talk about having other penchants, but being the boss, spanking when disobeyed for things like her safety and wellbeing was definitely his thing. She could handle it now that she had put a name to it. That was fine. She had a few kinks in bed as well. She wondered if he would explore them with her. On just a hook-up basis, nothing permanent, and even as she thought the words, she wished it didn't have to be that way. He could satisfy her through eternity.

"Hey sisterling, how goes it? You've been missing all day." Rafe leaned down and kissed the top of Piper's head but didn't wait for her response. "Smells good, Rosie. I don't get this type of food normally. Thanks for cooking." He dropped another kiss on his second sister's head.

"I'm just heating up some of the massive amounts of food people brought us and that is clogging the freezer. What's put you in such a good mood?"

"We just got an offer on the ranch."

"Really? That's great Rafe," said Rosie. "That'll take the burden off you, Piper."

"What? Wait, how did that come about? You can't sell without all of our signatures, Rafe."

"I know. I didn't commit. I just said I got an offer."

"Stop talking. I want to hear all about it when I can concentrate. Dinner is almost ready then we can chat." Rosie put her full concentration on finishing dinner while Piper stared without seeing her sister moving around in front of her.

They had barely sat down when Piper demanded Rafe talk. "Blackwell Investments came by and asked if we were interested in selling. I said we might be."

"That's it? What price did he offer?" Rosie asked.

Piper interrupted. "No, the first question you should be asking is why would he think that the place might be up for sale? Was he watching the obituaries or something? Had he already asked Pops?"

"That's what's funny about this whole thing. He said he had expected to talk to Pops. The two men were in suits and even asked if I were him."

"Something is fishy about this."

"What do you mean, fishy?" asked Rafe.

"As in, use your investigative mind. Something about this isn't right. Let me tell you why. I have an investment firm, so I know how it can go. I have fielded calls all week from my people sharing information and asking if they should do more digging, besides the normal everyday operation questions."

"So?" asked Rosie as she served food into a still empty plate in front of Piper.

"So, you know so much about your potential buy, you could impersonate them in your sleep and probably would beat out the actual person in believability."

Rafe followed Piper's line of thinking. "Which means that they would have known Pops passed away, that I was too young to be mistaken for him and lots more. He would have all the information instead of asking me the precise acreage and things."

"Right. I'm going to have my people look into this company." She started to pull out her phone when Rosie gave her the *mama bear* look. "After dinner," said Piper as she put the phone away.

Later that night, after she had put in the call to her office leaving information to be followed up on the next morning, she relayed the information to Jackson on his nightly visit. "Just as I suspected would happen. They approached Garth almost monthly for the last six months."

"What? This same company? Wait, I need to get Rafe because if I tell him, he will think I just want them to let me make a go of it. He needs to hear it from you."

"We've already talked about it."

"You've already talked about what?"

"Rafe and I have already discussed this offer. It was before your afternoon scuffle with the fence and while you were out with Andy."

"Nice of you to tell me, that was two days ago."

"Uh, sweetheart, we were busy first with you, and then, you were gone, and well this is later. Besides, Rafe said he wanted to mention it to you first."

"Well, we aren't selling."

"Fine, I told you I wanted first option if you did. You agreed."

"I know, but I want to try to make this a go. I have some information to wait for and this is the hard part. When you know you want to acquire, but need every little bit of information out there before you make a move."

"I know all I need to know to decide to make a move on you, sweetheart." Jackson leaned in to meet Piper's soft lips. "Glad you feel better. Now I can do this." He murmured as he deepened the kiss. When he lifted his head, they were both breathing heavier.

"Mmm, good to know I passed the first round of scrutiny." Piper smiled at Jackson.

He leaned down to punctuate his response with kisses. "And the second and the third."

She groaned. "You need to get to sleep. I have some company business to handle and then I need to go to bed. Besides, you don't want to just hook up and I am too busy to do more than that right now. Maybe ever."

Piper felt her inner boss rise up when Jackson spoke again, ignoring her last statement. "You shouldn't be working tonight after hitting your head the other day. I'm not going to have you get a headache because you refused to allow your body time to stabilize again."

"I'm not a kid any more who needs a big brother to take care of her. I'm fine."

"Good thing because I'm the furthest from a big brother that you will ever come across."

"I drove into Austin. If there was a problem, that is when you should have stepped in."

"If I'd known you were going, I might have. Now do as I say, because it's being kind to your body not because I'm going to roast your rear if I find out you haven't."

His intense kiss meant business just as his words expected compliance. Piper examined her choices and decided she was going to do better by agreeing and then doing what she wanted. It is how she was able to get where she wanted in business. Agree there is merit in other pathways, but when the right avenue opened, jump at it.

"Fine, but don't get used to winning with me, Jackson Knight."

"Yes, ma'am, I'll remember that." One last kiss and he was striding for the door. Just as he placed his hand on the knob he said, "And for the record, I use similar strategy for something I want. I don't hook up unless I have an end goal in mind."

Chapter 7

The next morning, as Piper was poring over the books in her father's office, she found some information on the previous offers in his calendar. Her cell rang. It was her office manager, Leanne. She listened then hung up and checked the clock. Lunch time had come and gone but she might be able to find her brother and sister close-by. She had things they needed to hear.

Once gathered in the living room, beverages of choice close at hand and more of the cinnamon rolls that Rosie had made for breakfast, Piper began.

"First off Rafe, I don't appreciate you treating me like you did last night, as though you didn't understand that there had been multiple offers made to Pops. You acted like the information was all new. I am shooting straight from the hip with the two of you, I expect the same courtesy."

"You're right. I just wanted to see your reaction. Sorry, Pips, I won't do it again."

"I know that you two are worried about me taking on this place."

"Well, not that you can't handle it. If anyone can do it, you can," assured Rafe. "What we're worried about, if we are shooting straight, is that you might take on the ranch out of obligation rather than honest desire."

Rosie jumped in. "Your plate is already overflowing with your own business. And we know you Piper."

"What do you mean you know me? You don't know me." She turned to Rosie. "You think I have a little business that makes enough money for me to live."

Rosie scrunched her face but didn't say anything. "I have a business that supports forty-seven full time and a handful of part time employees. We also have at least one but often two interns from Baylor Business or UT Austin."

Rosie's eyes grew. "You have that many employees. Even Tony doesn't have that many."

"I'm an investment and acquisitions firm. We don't need many to create big impact. And for anyone who doesn't have time to look me up, upwards of a billion dollars cross my desk every quarter. We have gone public this year so we have a standing on the stock exchange now. If that qualifies as little then I guess you are right. I call it success."

Rafe wove his pen over and under his fingers in a characteristic sign of stress. "Piper, we understand you work hard and are good at what you do. You are successful and know your stuff but what I think Rosie means is we know you overload and then you blow."

"What? That was when I was a kid and neither of you were around for much of that time."

At some point, Jackson knocked, walked in, and leaned in the entryway. He spoke up at this point. "That was the old Piper. The new Piper has more of a slow burn."

Piper gave him a disbelieving look, but she couldn't deny it. She normally had little implosions throughout each day. Finally, when she got to the end of her wick and the fuel was all but gone, she'd explode. She hadn't done it in a while, but she could feel it simmering.

"Regardless," said Rafe, "it's that explosion that we worry about."

"Rosie, I know you want Rafe to agree with you and sell the ranch, but I have some information that means we can't sell. Not right now. Or, if you do, I'll buy you out." Piper stood up to wander to the front window and Jackson straightened to amble over to sit in one of the recliners.

"What do you have? What have you learned?" Rosie was anxious again and Piper hated that. She would try to show them that they didn't have to worry. She could handle things.

Piper turned around and looked at her siblings and Jackson. "As you know, I spoke to my office and had them do some research on the ranch, the property, you know, all normal things I do when looking at an investment. The next thing is I had them check into Blackwell Investments." She paused to sit back on the sofa and pull out her notes.

"First, that investment company has had a number of questionable press releases, and while they have made some good deals, they sold all of them to a development company that ruined the feel of the areas they developed. For instance, if they bought this place they would put in apartments, or a cattle yard, or something. I don't think any of us wants that."

Piper knew how to present so she let that information settle before she continued. "That company has also been in the middle of several litigations and accused of shady practices."

"What kind of shady practices?" asked Rafe.

"The kind I would think needed an investigative reporter to check on. There were reports of things like property damage, one place's well-established dam was destroyed mysteriously overnight, causing the landowner to sell rather than go bankrupt because he lost all of his crops. It was ruled unlikely a natural occurrence, but there was no way to be definitive as to what actually did happen."

"Oh, Piper, that's just a coincidence. You're brighter than that," scoffed Rafe.

"Odd things happen all the time," Rosie admonished.

"I think I would equate the dam break to the hay field's irrigation lines to be destroyed overnight when there was no weather to cause it. Blackwell had been trying to purchase that land for over five years before the dam exploded. Once that happened, the company was on their door the very next day with another offer. Lower than the first."

"Well they offered me a very good price. More than I know the land is worth."

"And do you ask yourself why?"

Blackwell bought that one property and sold to a developer. The property is now a strip mall among other things."

Rafe stood up and paced the family room. "Piper, that is one incident."

"Hold on I have more. Another had a controlled burn of their lower fields attended by the local volunteer fire department. They certified the fire was completely out. In the night, a fire burned all of the outbuildings and stables and destroyed a good portion of the owner's home. Again, while it appeared that it was unlikely from other unavoidable events, there was no way to prove it except the fire department said it was not from the controlled burn. Again, Blackwell was actively trying to purchase the place and again the owners sold quickly."

"If it were suspicious, don't you think that some law enforcement would be looking at them? Local if not state and larger?" pointed out Rafe.

"Yes, of course, if there were any way that they could prove that it was something, but remember, the owners sold and left. They didn't protest or anything. There are less dramatic complaints of harassment and the like. Pops had notes on his calendar as recently as two weeks ago that said Blackwell. It isn't rocket science to know that is a note of contact."

"Yes, I told you that they had been visiting him almost monthly for a while," Jackson added. "He said they were not taking his refusal well, and were getting a little pushy. In fact, he asked if I would come over the next time they came. Just for a witness, you know?"

Rafe stood up in response to his agitation. "Why didn't Pops tell us?"

Jackson shrugged. "He said you were all so busy and I was just down the road. It was convenience most likely."

Piper jumped in. "This next bit of information that my people uncovered might be where you will want to focus some investigation, Rafe." She waited for him to reseat himself. "So, about a year ago, there was a man who had refused Blackwell Investments quite loudly. He made sure everyone around him knew he would not sell. Normally, that would be the end of it because in this business, your reputation is the most valuable asset you own. But it didn't seem to slow them down. Little things seemed to go wrong on his place. Finally, when he threatened to call the sheriff for trespassing if they returned, the visits stopped."

"See," said Rosie, "nothing wrong with that."

"Except that the man was dead with no apparent cause of death less than a month later." Piper sat back and expected to see some ah ha faces, but nothing happened. Piper jumped up. "Don't you wonder if they had something to do with it? I mean the man wasn't even sixty years old. No apparent reason for death."

"Baby, I know this is sounding like your daddy's situation, but it's just something that happens. I'm cautious but not convinced."

Rosie jumped up. "What? You think this is what happened to Pops? No way, no freaking way are you going to make his death any more than it was: a tragedy. Piper Gentry, this is hard enough as it is without you making up shit."

Piper opened her mouth and then shut it. Her sister never swore. It was unladylike.

"Sorry, Rosie, I got carried away. Forgive me. Don't cry. I'm sorry, really."

Rafe beat her to their sister and wrapped his arms around her in comfort. Jackson got up and snagged Piper around the waist, sitting in her discarded seat with her on his lap. She struggled to pull out but he tightened his hold and leaned in to her closely.

"Piper, we need to talk about this but not here. Your sister isn't going to be able to see any of it clearly. She just wants it all to be over and go home. I don't blame her. I know you have a plan. I could see you weren't finished talking. Give me your plan later. I'll be your sounding board for feasibility, all right? You need to preserve your relationship with these two."

She nodded her head and leaned back into him for a moment before sitting up. "Rosie, don't worry, I won't mention it again. You're right. I'm just tired, that's all."

Rosie nodded. "I know. We're all tired. I'm going to call Tony now if you're done."

"I am. Let him know we miss him here." Rosie nodded again and left the room.

Rafe sat back down and sighed. "I don't want to say any more to Rosie, but I don't think we want to deal with those people, Pips."

"No, I agree. What do you say we just let it go? I'll have all I need to make a decision tomorrow. Then everyone can go back to what they need to do. Rosie goes home day after tomorrow anyway. And I know you have things you want to do before you go off on this next assignment."

Jackson said, "If your information is correct, you're not getting into any dealings or mess with those people, Piper. You hear me on that."

Piper knew that he was just trying to protect her but to openly shut her down had never been the best approach with her.

"Jackson, I'm a grown-ass woman with plenty of experience working with people on the edges of the law."

"Companies that kill people, maybe even Garth?" Jackson demanded.

"Whoa, Pips, you don't really believe that they did something to Pops, do you?"

"I'm cautious over that, Rafe. I'm not at all sure or you can be damn sure I'd be hounding the police. I don't even know if there was enough of a reason anyway. I mean, there are plenty of places near here that would be ready to sell. It has been a hard few years."

Jackson quickly pointed out the obvious. "We don't know that they haven't sold out already."

"But you said they came here but not your place. I mean, we're side by side," Rafe pointed out.

"Yes, but we are three strapping men who don't show any signs of not being able to take care of our property. Garth was one man and while he had good workers, it is lonely sometimes and certainly less to work for if you're living alone. You know?"

"We didn't neglect him, Jackson." Piper said indignantly.

Rafe hung his head while he took a deep breath. "Well, Piper didn't, but I know I did and even if Rose lives out of the country, she could have called. I know she rarely did."

"It's no use rehashing it now and I can tell you he bragged on his kids every chance he got. Garth was proud of what each of you was doing."

Piper stepped out of Jackson's embrace and hugged Rafe. "On everything else, let's talk about it later. I obviously need to do some additional research and I have office work of my own to get to but if you agree that we don't have any further conversation with Blackwell, then that issue is settled."

Piper was determined to find out as much as she could about Blackwell Investments' interest in the ranch. Rafe had said they gave him a good offer. She wondered how good. She'd have to remember to ask him.

Out on the porch before leaving, Jackson, who had been burning his candle at both ends, kissed Piper and told her so.

"I know it's partly my fault. You've been great, but you can't keep this up. Go home, sleep, work, and visit with your brothers. I have a lot to do here as well. Rosie and Rafe leave soon so I need to get my ducks in a row."

"I know you're worried about Blackwell but if we simply continue to say no, soon they'll turn around and go somewhere else."

"Until they don't. Pops kept saying no, and they still came back. I think I'm going to have a gate installed and connect the fencing to it. It will stop them from walking onto the property like they have."

"That sounds like a good idea. On the subject of access, I don't think they would kill for the land."

"Yeah, I'm sure you're right, but things just sound fishy, you know?"

Jackson leaned down, his lips touching her again. "Stay out of trouble, woman."

She gave him a mischievous grin. "I'll try."

Even if this attempt at a second chance went nowhere, it felt good to be fussed over even in a bossy, Jackson Knight kind of way.

The next morning found Piper on the back of a horse seeing some of the operation with Andy, wishing she had left the riding for one more day. Descriptions never quite fit the bill for her. Being a visual learner first, Piper often tried to see things so she could recall them later. As the two were wheeling their mounts around to head back to the house, she spied a small pile of kicked up dirt.

"Andy, what happened out there?" She pointed in the direction of the dirt.

"Armadillo, badger, coyote, coon, or we might have our-selves a colony of prairie dogs, who knows. I'll get one of the guys to fill it back in and take a better look.

"It looks like drilling has gone on in the middle of the pas-ture. Not something an animal has made, but man." Curious, Piper got closer and Andy seemed hesitant but followed be-hind. He was shaking his head as though she were wasting time.

Shrugging his shoulders, he finally said, "Your dad had some core samples taken for some reason. Some fool notion that there were valuable minerals under the property. It must have been here."

"It looks fairly recent. Why didn't you know where he had taken the samples from?"

"Yep, about a month ago, I think and I didn't dog Garth's footsteps."

"And what happened to the samples? Where did he send them?"

"That I don't know. Bet you could check his calendar and you'd find it or his property journal. Anything that went on of note, he logged into that journal."

"Okay, I'll check it out. Did Pops own the mineral rights?"

"I think he said he did but that didn't have anything to do with running the place so we never talked about those types of things."

"I—"

A loud bang split the calm like a truck backfiring or a shot gun. So intense, in fact, that a flock of birds startled from their perches, her ears rang, and her horse spooked. Trying to settle the little mare down proved more than her rusty horse skills could handle. She soon found herself hitting the ground hard.

After her last fall from the fence, she was not in good shape to handle another so soon. Her arms went up to cover her still bruised head.

Her fall forced a hard grunt from her gut. As she felt her hip and side slam into the ground, her first thought was, *Jackson is going to kill me.* Then *that's gonna bruise."* Immediately, Andy was there to offer his hand and after a few moments to get her bearings, she took his offer. She didn't think she'd broken anything, and as he helped her up, she was able to do it without much achiness. She took her reins from his outstretched hand.

Chapter 8

"**Y**ou all right, Miss Piper?"

She nodded her head but didn't speak, still getting steady.

"What was that?" she finally asked.

"Not a clue. Most likely a poacher or someone was shooting at game or worse, shooting at one of the herd. I'll get you back home and have someone handle your horse. Then I'll take a few hands and check around for signs of where it might have come from."

"It was close. Too close. Does this happen often?"

"Don't know that it's ever happened before. We've had a few poachers but this close to people in the field and in broad daylight, not as likely. Could be someone on the Clear Knight had a shot go wild."

"It would have had to go really wild."

Cody nodded. "Now come on, let's get you back to the house. Rafe or your Jackson will skin me alive if anything happens to you."

"I'm a grown woman, Andy."

He laughed. "Yes ma'am, with a couple of protective men watching out for you. If you add in Jackson's brothers, you'll be lucky to breathe."

Piper grunted. "Over-protective you mean."

Andy kept his smile. "Yes ma'am."

After they started the trek back to the house, Piper said, "I can get myself back and can take care of my own horse."

"You fell off your horse so soon after the last fall. You're bound to have something that needs tending."

"Probably, but I can handle it. We have to work together Andy and this isn't going to go well if we have to debate things every step of the way. Please, just go check things out. I can take care of me and my horse."

He hesitated. "If you're sure you're okay..."

She nodded. "You mean if I'm sure the guys won't come after you? I am."

"All righty then," Andy slowed, tipped his hat and rode off in another direction.

Piper watched her gait, keeping it to a walk so she didn't encourage another headache and rode into the horse barn. After getting things settled for her mare, she left her with extra oats and went inside the house feeling a limp coming on.

Walking into the kitchen Rosie ran into both of her siblings, Piper in a chair with her ankle up on the table. She'd banged it up somehow in her fall. Rafe was cleaning it like a pro.

"Hey, Rafe, you look pretty good doing that. Ever want a change in professions?"

"Nah, where'd you think I learn these skills, out in the field. Being a reporter, correspondent, or a foreign anything, makes you more resilient and resourceful. I learned this in the first trip. But I didn't bring the supplies. That cabinet over there," he pointed to a cupboard door that was still open slightly, "is full of all sorts of clean me and fix me up first aid things."

Piper broke in the conversation. "There was a shot or something while Andy and I were outside looking at the place that Pops had done some core samples. In the southwest grazing pasture, there were these small holes with dirt near them. I think there are some in a number of places. I'm going to send hands out tomorrow to see if they can locate any more. We were about to look at the ones we found when we heard a loud bang. My horse spooked. I fell off." She indicated her ankle with a sweep of her hand.

Rafe nodded his head in the direction of Piper's leg, "It's not that long of a cut but it's a little deep so I'm hoping she can keep it clean long enough for it to begin healing from the inside out. Otherwise there might be some infection and it's just deep enough to cause a problem if that happens."

Rafe looked into Piper's face taking on that big brother stance and said, "And Piper's going to be a good girl and follow her big brother's advice, right?"

Piper groaned her irritation, rolling her eyes for affect. "You do know I run an international company with multiple employees, right?"

"And you do know," inquired Rafe, "that I will always be the big brother thereby the boss of you?"

Rosie reached over and patted Rafe on the shoulder. "Only at the family dinner table dear, Piper has proven she can take care of herself, usually."

"What does that mean?" asked an already offended Piper.

"What it means dear sister is that you do too much for too long for too many people and you get overloaded. It means that you work too many days in a row without a break, too many hours in a day without help, and you take on too many things without taking something else off your plate to balance it. This ranch is a perfect example."

Rosie pulled a chair out next to Piper and grabbed her hand with both of hers as she sat leaning into her sister to make her point.

"Rosie you don't know what you're talking about. I have plenty of help that I pay well for. I don't do too much because if I did then I would be a basket case and everything would fall down around my ears, which is not happening. I do balance things. I simply have a different center of gravity than you and it means that I can take on more things without other things tumbling off. Like this ranch."

Rafe caught Rosie's eye and did a short negative move of his head to indicate she needed to stop. They had all been down this road with Piper before and they all knew where the road ended. It ended with Piper getting upset and leaving early, Rosie crying, and until this visit, Rafe and his dad discussing quietly how to keep the girls civil to each other for a whole visit. They'd done really well on this one, but nerves were taut and the tension was thick. If they could last one more day, Rosie would be on her way back to her loving husband, a whole continent away.

"You're right Piper you've been able to do quite a few things that nobody would have thought a young woman of your age could accomplish," acknowledged Rafe. "And Piper," his tone was all about big brother edicts "it's not that we don't think you have a good head on your shoulders, that you can't handle your business. We believe you know when things are too much, but we also know how time-consuming and how big a project the ranch really is.

"Even Pops said the last visit that he thought that it was getting too much for him. So if you still want to keep the ranch, Rosie and I are just going to want a few promises." Rafe stood quiet for a moment watching Piper's response and just when it looked like she was going to say something, he added, "And I have discussed it with Jackson."

"You discussed what with Jackson?" Piper yanked her leg off the table and stood. "You have no right to bring Jackson in on family business especially when it is me you're talking about."

"Piper, you're dating him again, aren't you?" asked a confused Rosie.

"Yes, no, well, it remains to be seen. Regardless, he is not my decision maker. I am. How dare you go behind my back," Piper stopped when she saw both of her siblings look past her.

"Afternoon everyone, did I come at a bad time?"

Piper turned her head and looked Jackson in the eye. He held her stare until she looked away. His raised eyebrows and intense look told her that he had already heard something had happened.

"Nope, it's fine. You and my family here can talk about me all you want. I'm going to see what Andy found out about the poacher." She turned to go and big, rough hands attached to solid arms stopped her progress.

"What are you talking about?" Jackson demanded, his hand sliding suggestively to the camber of her bottom.

Piper sighed, understanding the message of caution he sent. She relayed the story for the third time, irritated when Rafe filled in some of the more worrisome details that Piper had skimmed over. She shot her brother an angry look. It was quiet for what seemed like an age but finally, the arms that held her released her.

One hand slipped over hers. "Will you excuse us? We have a few things to discuss."

"Sure, but since it seems like Piper is going to keep the ranch, and Rosie leaves early tomorrow and so do I, it might be better if we have this talk with all of us. Get the business out of the way. Okay, Pipsqueak?" Rafe leaned down and kissed the top of her head mussing it just a bit.

Piper was still somewhat miffed. "Cut it out, Rafe. I'm not a little kid anymore."

"I know, hon, I know but this visit you seem so much more approachable. You know, less distant and cold."

"That's what I said to Tony. You aren't all professional-like."

"Great. My family thought I behaved like a cold, emotionless shark before. Let's get it over with then."

"First I need to pull out things for lunch. I know it's only twelve, but people are always less cranky if they have a full tummy."

"Spoken like a true American married to an Italian," smirked Piper. The tension lessened slightly.

Rosie, with the reluctant help of Piper, pulled together some of the leftovers for lunch. They had been trying to eat up the food but finally, Rosie declared after breakfast this morning, she was going to wrap and freeze whatever they hadn't already frozen or pitch it out.

Lunch consisted of those non-frozen items now. She promised a meal made from scratch for their last dinner together. It would be a long time before the siblings would all be gathered again.

As the two girls worked in the kitchen, Piper addressed a concern of hers. "Rosie, do you think that a person could love someone for a long time but live without them? I mean, have a normal life without them."

"Is that what you think has happened between you and Jackson? You both have led a normal life and when thrown together, like this week, all your hidden feelings appear to have jumped out?"

Piper fidgeted with the plate of cold cuts and cheese. "I guess."

"How do you feel about leaving him and going back to Austin to stay?"

"It makes my stomach churn and head hurt. I feel frantic, but I'll have to do it, I mean, I have a company to run. In one way, I'm sure I'll be fine. But in another moment, I don't want to think about it because it hurts."

"Then I'd say, yes. Is that how Jackson feels?"

"Well the physical part of the pain, I've no idea, but he says he has known all along that he was in love with me. Seeing me this last week proves it to him."

"And do you believe him?"

"I want to, but I've had more than my share of men who say one thing to get what they wanted, usually to ride the wave of my success or baser needs fulfilled."

"I guess that would be a drawback to having a successful company. Having a substantial bank account. But don't you spend time with equally successful men? I mean those with their own prestigious companies?"

"Yeah, but I realized I needed to reassess my goals when the president of a marketing firm started calling me. I found myself calculating how I could use his business to boost mine. I was doing what others had done to me."

Piper stopped, afraid that she was revealing too much of herself. But if she couldn't tell her sister, there was no one to confide in. "The trouble was, I didn't know that he was the exception I had been looking for until it was too late. He wasn't playing a game. He was actually interested in me."

"Oh Pips, then what happened?"

Piper shrugged. "By the time I figured things out it was too late. He'd gone elsewhere, as he should have."

"Honey, I'm so sorry. It must be hard trying to decide if someone is interested in you or how your association can benefit them."

"Yeah, well last night one of the phone calls I received was from another gentleman, and whether his intentions were honorable or not, I'm too afraid of the possibility of it being a sham. I just can't be that gullible fish taking a bite on another man's baited line again only to find its plastic with a hook imbedded."

"I understand, but you can't think that's what Jackson is doing. He isn't trying to get to you for what you have of value to him."

"No, of course not, but I don't know if it's fair to get more serious. I mean, what if I can't give him what he deserves? I know how to be successful in business the problem is, what if I'm not profitable in anything else? I'm not successful in working in moderation or even close. I'm lousy at watching my diet or sticking to an exercise routine because those interfere with the prime objective, the company's success."

"Piper, do you think that you work too many hours because you think there isn't anything in your life besides the company? And if that's the case, do you want that kind of life? I'd think about it. I'd start reassessing my priorities before there isn't anything to consider besides a lonely existence." Rosie kissed her sister's cheek in a rare show of affection as she walked out of the kitchen carrying the luncheon platters. "Bring the tea, will you?"

"Yeah, sure," answered Piper. *I don't want to be that person anymore.* But she had no clue how to be anyone else. When she was a kid, she wanted to scale tall buildings, conquering them all. She thought she had. What do you do when you find that when you look around to share your triumphs and trials, you're the only one standing on the top of that pinnacle? It was cold and desolate standing in the spot you thought you wanted most in this world, alone. Could Jackson be that one to share it with or would he only be there on his terms? Could she compromise enough to make them both happy?

Sitting down to lunch, Piper said what she knew they all had figured out. "I'm keeping the ranch. I can make a good go of it. The numbers are good, the land is plentiful, and we have decided not to sell to the Blackwell Group, so I need to get down to business. We need to step up the productivity, but Andy will help with that."

Rafe began building his sandwich. "But how are you going to do that with your company?"

"I'll have to divide my week but right now, I will do most of the work from here until I'm sure things are able to run smoothly without me. Then I'll have to split my week between

Austin and here. I'll do Monday through Thursday in Austin. Thursday night through Sunday I'll be here."

"And the poacher?" asked Rosie.

"Not sure if there was one. I haven't had the time to ask Andy but he wasn't concerned so I should be less concerned." Piper reached for tomato slices.

"No one should be shooting in broad daylight on your property but you, Piper," warned Jackson.

"Well, sure, so we need to be more cautious and more aware," Piper responded.

Rafe added, "No doing anything stupid. You let the men you hire do the work you pay them to do. It's not good business to pay a person for a job and do the job for them."

"Good point, Rafe. I promise to let them do the work they should be doing. As soon as I figure out what each of them is hired to do."

They all ate for a few moments and then Rosie spoke up. "Now, tell me about those holes in the ground you found?"

"Oh, Andy said those were where the core samples were taken. There's some in the south pasture and probably other places. Rafe, do you know if we have the mineral rights to this land?"

"Should. We've both had the land since the late nineteenth century before there was a town."

"Well, I'm going to the land office and pull the records. Seems to me that Pops wouldn't have done core samples unless he knew he had the rights."

"But why now? The ranch isn't in trouble financially," asked Rosie.

Jackson had stayed predominately quiet as Garth's children discussed what they should do with the ranch and how it was going to work. Even at their worst, the Gentrys were a much more civilized lot when discussing things than his family. They had differing opinions, but words were found to express their disagreements. He and his brothers would nearly come to blows at times. The mineral tests made him curious.

"I wonder why Garth never told me about the samples. Where did he send them or have them sent?"

"I don't know yet, but I aim to find out. Okay, I need power of attorney from you two. I need you to sign a document that allows me to run the ranch and make the operating decisions. I won't sell or trade without consulting with you two and getting a three-way agreement. I can use the same paper for the operating document as well. I probably won't need it but I just want to make sure no one can challenge me. I'll record it when I do a title and document search."

"Good," said Rosie, "because I have plenty on my end of the world to take care of already. Worrying about any day-to-day problems with the ranch would not make me happy or be practical."

"Right, and with me out of the country as well, it will make things easier."

"I had my legal department draw up a general all-purpose document that only requires two non- related witnesses. Jackson I'll need you and Andy to witness the signatures since I can't notarize something pertaining to me."

"I'll clean up the table while Rafe runs to get Andy."

"Good because Piper and I need to step into the office for a conversation," said Jackson as he threaded his fingers with hers, pulling her into the room.

Chapter 9

Jackson shut the door behind them and pulled Piper into a kiss that tasted of irritation and relief. "When I heard you had a poacher that shot near you in broad daylight and you fell off your horse, my heart stopped. What were you doing so far out on a horse so soon after falling and banging your head?"

"Slow down cowboy. I needed to go out and I'll have to go again. Jackson, you don't think that I can leave everything to others on the ranch, surely."

"No, of course not, but you have to use your better judgement. You didn't do that today."

"I didn't know that someone was going to shoot near us or poach or that the horse was going to spook."

"No, I guess not. You aren't to go out there alone. It's too dangerous now that there's a poacher. Why'd you come back alone not knowing who or what was shooting? That was a damn fool thing to do and you could have gotten yourself killed."

It was obvious to Piper that Jackson was trying to control his responses and having a tough time of it. He was pissed at her and she knew it.

He let go of her to pace the small open floor.

"Fine, I wasn't there alone, and I won't ride that far alone if I can help it but Jackson, you need to get a grip."

"I've just got you back. I'm not risking anything happening to you. Andy should have never let you go home alone."

"I convinced him you wouldn't come after his hide if he let me come in while he checked out the source. I practically refused to allow him to follow along. Besides, there was a better chance of him finding who it was if he could gather more people and go quickly instead of getting me home first. It was time we couldn't afford to waste."

"Nevertheless, I'm going to have me a talk with Andy and there are going to be better safeguards in place."

She reached up and kissed him. "Thank you for caring, and be kind to Andy. He was trying to do what he thought you and Rafe would want but I didn't let him."

He grunted and kissed her hard again. "Now bend over the arm of the sofa."

"What? I will not." Piper took a step back but was hindered from going further by the large desk behind her.

"You heard me, over the arm of the sofa. You are never to allow yourself to be vulnerable like that again. Understood?"

Worry laced her words. "But, I was fine. It's more dangerous in Austin at night than walking or riding in the south pasture."

"Another problem, but we won't address that today. Today you came to no harm. This time. But what about next time? No, you need to understand how much I love and care about you."

He led her to the sofa and placed his hand between her shoulder blades, gently but firmly pushing her upper body over the arm down to the sofa cushion.

"I promise to be more cautious next time. Jackson, don't." Her words sounded watery. "I couldn't have known."

"Yes ma'am, I hear you and hope you're telling the truth, but you're going to feel my hand. Next time I promise you will feel more than that."

He grabbed the waistband on her riding pants and pulled both pants and panties down to her knees. Jackson swatted her hands away when they tried to cover the apple of her bottom cheeks now on display.

He wasted no time slapping those cheeks, one, two, three rub. He repeated the same pattern on her other side. Then his hand landed on her bottom hard, solid, and incessant. Piper quickly lost count and began to plead with her disciplinarian.

"Please, Jackson, I'm sorry. I won't ever do it again. I promise. It hurts," she squealed.

He stopped and rubbed her bottom. Piper knew to wait him out. It had been years since she had received a punishment spanking from Jackson but some things a woman doesn't forget. He wasn't really punishing her, but irrationally trying to create a ring of cognitive safety around her. He loved her.

She allowed him to comfort her as he wanted and she craved. She knew that when he ran his finger through her hot channel, it would be red and flooded. Piper never understood her body's reaction to his corrections, whether verbal or physical but she always reacted the same way. She should be boiling angry but she was aroused beyond belief.

His voice was gentle, almost cooing when he spoke to her. "I love you sugar and I'm so afraid for you to be here alone." He pulled her up and wiped her unshed tears with his thumb, kissing her cheeks and eyes.

"I know but I can make this ranch profitable like it used to be. Right now, it isn't doing much more than breaking even. That's fine if it's a simple living we want but the potential is so much more. But you know ranching. Sometimes, without you doing anything different or unsafe, it will be physically challenging and risky."

"I understand so long as you understand that I'm not going to let you be reckless. I know that isn't what happened today until you sent Andy off before you got to the house. Daddy loves you so damn much. I get scared your bravado will get you into a fix you can't get out of." He pulled strands of her hair behind her ear. "Hear me now." His tone hardened. "If you are out there without protection, you're going to feel caring of another kind. You get me? I'll bring out the kind of caring made of leather."

"I can't agree that you can smack my butt for going against you, Jackson."

"Yeah, well that's too bad because you know it will happen. No excuses or explanations will be enough. This is your last warning. I don't make a big production of spankings like I did today. I just do them and go on."

"I remember," she said with annoyance. "So long as you remember I can scream."

He leaned and kissed her hard again. "Good, we've come to an understanding, and baby cakes?"

"Hmm?"

"I'm so relieved that you weren't hurt. I won't have to go on a rampage to find and dispose of the shooter. Rearranging my schedule would have been a challenge." He grinned. "Now let me kiss it and make it better. It'll have to be quick though."

"Yes, please," she moaned as Jackson's hand returned to her southern end and touched the sensitive center.

He draped her over the back of the sofa. Piper shivered. It wasn't long, with his member hard as diamonds pushing against her outer realm and the sound of wetness in her pussy, that she was reaching her peak. Her hot ass rubbing against the cloth of his jeans, his skillful finger action, and demanding lips on her pulse spot behind her ear and on the column of her neck, sending tremors of arousal through her. He put her over, crashing on the jagged land below. It was so good, so damn good.

"Jackson, I need more."

He kissed her once more before coming up for air. "I know baby but not tonight. Tomorrow, you'll have the house to yourself. We can work on more then."

Her pout and grunt of dissatisfaction earned her a loud smack to her cooling butt.

"Fine, but I'm holding you to that, mister." She rubbed her bottom.

"Yes ma'am." Jackson grinned as he pulled her pants and panties up into their original position.

Piper giggled and grabbed the paperwork as Jackson led her out of the room kissing her ear. She didn't know where the giggle came from. She didn't giggle even as a love-sick teen. She shook her head but couldn't be upset really. She had experienced the first physically induced orgasm by a living breathing man in longer than she wanted to admit. She felt wonderful if not achy, wanton and only partially fulfilled.

When Piper and Jackson reappeared in the family room, Rosie, Rafe, and Andy were there waiting along with one of the hired hands. Rosie avoided looking in their direction fully and Rafe gave Jackson a hard stare which he blithely ignored. Rafe looked between the couple and opened his mouth several times to say something and then didn't.

"So, do you have those papers?" Rafe asked his red-faced sister.

Relieved that he didn't say what she was sure was on his mind, Piper went into the safer CEO mode.

"Yes. Let me show you each where to sign. Hello Dan, what can I do for you?"

"I decided I wanted Jackson on here to be someone who could make a decision if you weren't available for some reason. Emergency basis, but now," Rafe looked at the two still standing near each other, "I'm not sure."

"No, that's a great idea. Jackson, if you're willing to be my second, so to speak, I'd appreciate it."

"If that's what you want."

Rafe and Rosie spoke simultaneously. "It is."

Piper nodded. "Okay then, let me call my lead attorney."

"You have him on speed dial and he takes your calls?" asked Rosie.

"I employ him. Of course, he takes my calls."

"Hi, Rashid, sorry to call unannounced but I have a question."

And in a few moments, the addition was added and coming over her fax.

"I'm impressed," said Rafe.

"I told you I run a corporation. If I want to play golf in half an hour, I could get a helicopter to drop me at a club that I don't belong to and I'll have permission and entry tickets waiting for me."

Rafe shook his head. "I guess I didn't think of you other than my baby sister who had a business."

"I did tell you that you had no clue."

Rosie said with sudden dawning, "You are rich, I mean filthy rich."

"By some standards I suppose I am, but let's not dwell on that. It makes me uncomfortable."

"I know, but Piper, I had no idea." Rosie took a step back as though she shouldn't stand too close to Piper.

"I told you there was so much more to me than you knew. But I'm your family, Rose Gentry Morelli, not some balance sheet so cut it out. Quit looking at me like that."

Piper slapped her stack of papers on the table. Jackson came up behind her, sharing his heat and strength, placing his hands over hers.

"Shh, sweetheart, be calm and breathe. She didn't mean to hurt you. It surprised her, that's all."

Piper took another breath, sighed, and nodded. "Okay, let me read this out loud so everyone hears the changes and agrees to them. She spread out the paperwork on the ever-present coffee table her parents had insisted on keeping in the family room. Today she was glad they had. Her siblings read the papers carefully at Piper's suggestion and she produced copies for them to take home.

"I can email you a copy of the signed document as soon as I get back to Austin this week."

"Piper, you have us each getting one third of the profits but is that really fair if you're doing the work?"

"Sure Rafe. From now through the second quarter, there won't really be much profit to share. I'll need to reinvest it all into upgrades and the like for the first six months. Then I'll see about third quarter. But by fourth quarter next year, you should see a decent check coming in and from then on, it should be the same."

"Well, do what you need to do, but if the ranch can't do more than break even, I don't think the work is worth it."

"I agree Rosie, but we have to give it some time to recover the loss of Pops."

"How long are you looking to work before it should show a profit and if it doesn't you will look for a buyer?"

"So some ROI, profit to pocket, in a year is the goal. However, I have the plan broken down on the sixth page. It states how I will figure profits, how much reinvestment will occur and the like. And even if it isn't for profit, I might purchase the property outright, buy you out."

Piper had laid down extra copies for Andy and Jackson to read and when Jackson sat back, having read the whole, he smiled.

"Because you can," said Rosie softly.

"Yes, because I can. I'm not apologizing for having made good investments of time and money. Nor do I expect to be treated differently by any of you because I have." Piper looked around the room.

Rafe spoke before anything else could be said. "You did a great job of it, Pips."

"It was my contract person who pulled it together but thanks." She looked around the room. "Do you have any questions that I didn't cover on the agreement?"

Her siblings sat back shaking their heads. "Nope, I think it's good," agreed Rafe.

Piper laughed. "Just pulling this paperwork together, I found that Pops' office was one that was more for last century than this one. I'll have to put some reliable office equipment in so I can conduct business from here for both endeavors. I'm putting in a satellite dish. I'm having my guy explore the best options. We're isolated out here as far as technology goes. News is important to me and while Pops was happy with one station, I need more. I need to do conferences and things, as well. I hope that's okay with everyone."

The murmurs of agreement floated around the room before she asked if they were ready to sign their documents.

"Okay, there's an initial line on every page at the bottom right, you two, sorry three, initial every page there and then a signature on the last page. After everyone signs, Dan and Andy you sign. Use your legal names so not Dan and Andy but Daniel and Andrew."

"It's really Danny."

"Danny? Sorry, I assumed, and that was wrong of me. I should have known better." She took the paperwork out of the "boardroom" feel and brought it back into their front room. The tension lessened.

"Jackson, Rosie and I have a brotherly request of you and Andy." Rafe looked over at Piper who suddenly was very interested.

Jackson leaned back draping his arm along the back of the sofa behind Piper and cupped his hand along her neck. He slid his palm up to the base of her head and wove his fingers into her hair, massaging the area. Piper remembered his old technique of keeping her in place so she wouldn't leave before he was ready, before she had listened to what she needed to hear. She leaned back, prepared not to like what she was going to hear from Rafe.

Rafe lifted his eyebrow as though surprised that he got no complaints from Piper, but he continued. "I know Piper said she would spend half the week in Austin and half here but we all know or most of us do anyway, that Piper jumps into a project with both feet and doesn't emerge until she's satisfied."

Piper knew where this was going. "Rafe, I'm going to be fine."

"Well, I want some insurance. If you stay here and work at the ranch, I want someone here helping you stay out of trouble, that's Andy. I also want someone to make sure that you are safe at night, that's going to be Jackson."

"What? You want Andy to babysit me in the day and Jackson at night? Are you mad?"

Rafe shrugged. "Call it what you will, Pips, but I'm serious. I, *we* want Jackson to sleep here when you are on the ranch and Andy to keep an eye out when you're working on the Ranch."

"Might I remind all of you that I own—"

"Your own company, we know. With security, alarms, and the like, but here it's different. There is nothing between you and harm except what we put in place and that is going to be two men. Honey, please?"

Piper forgot the hand in her hair and she tried to stand up. Jackson put his free hand on her arm and caressed as he rubbed the scalp under her hair that had pulled in her attempt to rise.

"Jackson, let me up." Her hand went to cover his at her neck.

He leaned in to speak in her ear. "No. You're going to sit here and listen unless we need to take a short break and administer another lesson. Is that what we need to do? Rafe has the right to expect you to listen to him."

Piper slammed her head back against his hand on the back of the sofa as her answer. She hoped it smashed his tool of bondage. "Fine, Andy can help me if I need it on the ranch and Jackson can spend the night if he wants when I'm here."

"Actually, I had a talk with Jackson, Walker, and Sawyer yesterday and they all agreed that Jackson should stay the nights here period because it isn't good to have the house empty. He'll work his ranch but come here afterwards."

Piper was sullen. "I don't cook whole meals because I work too... um, I microwave."

"No problem," shared Rosie, "you have tons of frozen leftovers that I put in meal portions. Also, I put a few more meals in there that you could microwave or toss in the oven. You can grab things from the freezer section at the grocers when you need more."

Jackson smiled. "Thanks Rosie, but I can and do cook."

"Thank goodness one of you will. I won't worry as much now that I know she won't be having grocery store salads every meal she remembers to take. Worse yet, chips, cookies and diet soda."

"Shut up, all of you just shut up. I know how to cook, I just don't like to and I don't have time to waste doing it. And I'm not a child, Rafe."

"No you're not, but you're my baby sister and if you don't agree, then we will not agree for you to run the place." Rafe leaned back and intertwined his fingers, putting them behind his head. "So, what'll it be, Pips?"

"Fine, fine, but when will I be old enough for you to let me do what I want without needing an escort or babysitter, or whatever? Forty maybe? Because it's obvious that thirty isn't."

"I hate to tell you this, Piper Kay, but that is never going to happen until you get married as far as I'm concerned. Sorry, I know it's chauvinistic of me, but there it is. You were Pop's and my responsibility and now you're just mine."

"Well, baby cakes, looks like we are all in agreement." Jackson leaned down and kissed her. "I need to get going. Sorry to see you go, man, but we'll talk." Jackson shook Rafe's hand and leaned over to kiss Rosie's cheek. "And you call as soon as you are home, understand?"

Rosie blushed. "I'll let everyone know I'm home."

"Right, walk me out, baby?"

"Do I have a choice?"

"Tonight, yes." She walked out with him anyway and he drew her close when they got on the porch. Andy walked past them, shaking Jack's hand and went to his little house on the property.

"Jackson, I'm going to make this work."

"I know baby, I want you to."

"And it isn't dangerous."

"Piper, listen, we love you. All of us, but we know you. It's true, I'm just learning your more recent habits but most of you is the same woman I left at the university all those years ago, and most certainly the same woman I knew had stolen my heart. So, if we seem a little overprotective then so be it. Rafe is feeling the push to protect his baby sister now more than ever.

But it isn't new. He has had some pretty demanding conversations with me over the years when we were in high school. That's why I didn't ask you to marry me when you graduated. He wanted you to experience life outside of the ranch and I agreed. Garth wasn't as happy about it, but Rafe was right."

Jackson drew Piper into his arms and kissed her, his rigid shaft pressed hard against her belly leaving no doubts of his need. "Now we have a second chance and I'm taking it. I love you. I really love you but I'm not going to push anything because we need time, and now we have to figure this ranch out."

"*I* do. *I* have to figure things out on the ranch, not you."

"Okay, *you* need to work on this project and I want to watch you do it, help if I can. We have time for the rest. That is, if you want the time."

"I want the time. Just, Jackson? Don't suffocate me."

"You got it. You're in charge of the timing, for now." He kissed her again. "Don't take too long or I'll have to take over. Yeah?"

She reached up and kissed him in return. "Yeah."

Jackson leaned back. "I don't want you to speak with those Blackwell people without me. I'm firm on that and you have to promise me."

"I said that I'd be careful."

"You did, but that isn't the same thing. You know what I want."

"Me?" Her eyes sparkled in their merriment.

"Yes, but if you don't call me if they come back and then wait for me, what I will get is you, over my knee. Capisce?"

"Great, you're expanding your horizons by being bossy in two languages."

Jackson kissed her hard and swatted her butt, before leaving her yearning for more than the pressing of lips. "Just remember," he said.

She turned around and spent the last hours with her family before heading up to bed and staying awake even later, working on her schedule and to do list. Gate, ranch hand meeting, call for assistant...

Chapter 10

Piper changed into wranglers, before grabbing her hat, slipping her feet into her work boots, and striding out of the kitchen door letting the screen slam behind her. She laughed at the memory of how many times her mom would yell after the kids and her dad for slamming the door on the way outside. Piper mentally shrugged her shoulders. She didn't know how else to shut a screen door. She'd be willing to argue it just didn't shut any other way.

Her mind turned to the ranch and all the things that she loved about growing up on the land as she went to the stables to saddle Sparkle, the mare who had claimed the young executive cowgirl as hers.

As she rode the perky mare, Piper cleared some of the emotional sadness and cobwebs out of her mind. She still had many moments throughout the days that reminded her of the man who protected her from the day he knew she was going to be his, until the day he died.

She hadn't told anyone that he'd called her the day before he died and asked her to come that weekend. She said she would do the best she could to make it. Pops had mentioned Jackson for some reason and that he thought he was a good man. Said he enjoyed his company.

Well, she had made it that weekend, but it was to bury him, not visit. Rafe had taken Rosie to the airport the morning after they signed the paperwork and gone on to his place at College Station, about an hour from the ranch. The ranch had always been the middle ground for she and Rafe, each living about an hour on each side of it. Now even Rafe was out of the country.

Piper was devastated the day he flew out, and she cried all day. She was all alone. It was as though Jackson knew, because he was there a few hours after Rafe's flight.

He took one look at her blotchy wet face and gathered her in his arms bringing on a new torrent of tears.

"Hey, baby, come here and let me cuddle with you. I know you feel deserted but you're not. I'm here for you, always."

Piper snuggled into his arms and proceeded to saturate his work shirt. He never said a word. When she had cried herself out, he sent her to take a bath and made scrambled eggs while she soaked. He helped her into bed afterwards, crawling in behind her, and held her all night. The next morning, she was awake early but not as early as he was.

He left her a note that said for her to call him when she got around. Piper had never loved that man more than she did that morning. He'd allowed her the comfort during the evening, and the gathering of her dignity the next morning. He hadn't asked for anything but that she allow him to be there for her. She didn't call him but later that morning, she texted him two words, *Thank you.*

That was a few weeks ago. Over that time, she'd begun to balance the sadness with some excitement of a new project. She felt the joy of new hope that maybe this was what she'd been looking for to settle her heart and give her some peace. Running both her company and the ranch had proven harder than she had first thought. She didn't let on that the extra work was a strain, but she had gotten the ever-resourceful Josie to help.

Josie was her office assistant on loan from her GWI staff, to help Piper see what an assistant was able to do at the ranch office while Piper was working the Austin office. It was working out to be one of the best decisions she could have made.

Now that things were in a manageable routine, she didn't need to admit the early difficulties. On the days she wasn't at one place she stayed in contact. She telephonically checked in at the ranch and video-conferenced the office as needed. She spoke to Andy daily and to Jackson several times a day. He insisted. She didn't mind, usually.

Piper rode along the trail sometimes galloping sometimes trotting, or walking, making notes in her head for things to talk to Andy about. She'd gotten some information on the core sample her Pops had taken before he died. After talking with her office about refining that information, she had begun to look at experts to help her.

That in progress, she turned her mind to livestock. Something caught her attention, and she saw movement out of the corner of her eye. *It's probably Jackson checking up on me.* She checked her watch. No, he was moving a herd today.

As she realized it was either a bear or a man ahead, she slowed to a walk. It was hot, and she forgot to bring water. Piper chastised herself for not remembering some of the basic things of being out on the ranch winter or summer. You brought your gloves, first aid kit, water, snack, gun, and your working cell phone. She drank her last water yesterday and didn't replenish. The men in her life would have added to her list that she shouldn't go alone.

Jackson had told her just yesterday, "You tell somebody where you're going and when you expect to be back. And you don't go too far alone."

Jackson would be tanning her hide if he found out she was this far from home without anyone knowing where she was today. The only thing that she'd remembered was some gloves and her cell phone. She grabbed the gloves because while her rear was acclimated to the saddle, her hands would always need protection.

She had her cell phone because she never went anywhere without it. The day after the run-in with the barbed wire, Jackson had gotten her hooked to the local tower without a new phone or number. It had worked ever since.

As she approached the object in the trail, she saw that it was a man. She hesitated. The closer she got she saw that familiar gait. It was Jackson. Why he wasn't moving cattle, she had no idea but saying she was looking for Andy and conducting business over the phone when no one knew her location would be a bad idea and just doing a quick ride of the eastern fence would be equally frowned on.

She felt a lurch of eagerness at the sight of that man in front of her. She had that same tummy tingle excitement whenever she saw him but today it was accompanied with that deep-down dread. Maybe, if she was careful, she would be able to change directions before he noticed her behind him.

Unfortunately, when he slowed to climb back on his horse, he must have heard her approach because he turned around before she could head in the other direction. He tipped his hat back and sat waiting for her to get to him.

While she didn't want to admit it, she knew she deserved what she was about to get. It caused her heartbeat to speed up just a little and her hands were beginning to sweat in the gloves. They were sweating so much that she pulled them off as soon as she drew up next to him and wiped her palms on her jeans.

"Hey, Pips, what're you up to?"

No matter what she said, she was not getting out of this easily, so she plowed on ahead.

"I'm just riding to clear my head, finished a conference call, and looking for Andy."

"I see. Does that mean you started out with him?"

"Nope."

"But you got a message to him that you were coming this way."

Piper watched her man sit so calm, patiently waiting for her answer. How did he do that? It was like he knew she was too far from home in the heat of the day. Andy would not have agreed.

"Nope."

"Hold on a sec." Jackson pulled his phone out of his hip pocket holder and looked at the screen, "Huh, I didn't get a message either."

"It's because I didn't send one."

"So, what would make you break our agreement and put your hind end on the line?"

"I have some stock conversations I need to have with Andy, and I got some information on the core sample Pops had done. I just finished an acquisition at GWI last night, drove here early this morning, and I'm bone tired. Following all of your edicts just isn't going to work for me today."

Piper had sat back in her saddle and cocked her head to the side just slightly with the bill of her hat obscuring part of her vision, but at his word she sat up straight and pushed her hat back a little, so she could clearly see all that was Jackson. She wanted to make her point that she was in charge of her choices, not him.

"You were there today? In Austin and at the lab where the core samples were processed?" His voice had taken on that edge of dominant irritation.

"I wasn't in either place for long. I just wanted to finish business before coming to the ranch and decided to come and count how many samples were taken so I knew how many to ask for. The guy at the lab that I talked to said he needed to ask some verification questions. Plus, I needed to bring proof I had the right to get the information. Otherwise, he intended to mail them to the house next week."

"Why didn't you just let him do that?"

"Curiosity. Besides, I'm not one to sit around waiting for information that is ready to share."

"It killed the cat, you know."

"Curiosity? Yeah, but satisfaction brought him back."

Piper grinned, and Jackson laughed heartily. "Yeah, that's you all over, isn't?" She shrugged. "Now back to the real issue at hand here young lady. Get off your horse, darlin.'"

"What? No, I won't get off my horse, Jackson, I'm too busy today. Today, *I'm* the boss and I don't need you interfering."

"Well, then you can just simmer on the worry until I get home tonight."

Piper unconsciously backed Sparkle up a few paces. "You aren't spanking me, Jackson Knight. Especially for doing what I said I would do, take care of business."

A slow wide grin broke out on Jackson's face. "Yessum, that is exactly what I intend to do. I had thought to get it over here and now as that is how I normally like to do it, but I can see that you need to stew on this a while. I'll get to you tonight."

Piper bit her lip and turned her head away to think. It might be easier to just give in out on the land. He would probably go easy because of the ride home and she could get back to her work.

Turning back, she had made a decision and huffed in annoyance.

"Okay, I'll get off my horse."

"No, ma'am. I have work to do. I'll get to you later."

Piper knew it would be excruciating if she had to wait for her punishment. "It is now or never, mister."

"Don't worry, baby cakes, I'll get to you tonight. I'd recommend you get back home now before I add to this little punishment you have earned."

She hated how smug and confident that man was. And she loved the trickle of excitement and dread he gave her. Piper couldn't believe she was about to beg him to spank her so she didn't have to wait. She hated to wait. Patience was not her virtue.

She needed to get a grip. He wouldn't spank her at all. She was an adult, damn it and while it was enticing as a teen, it was not anything of the sort now. She hoped she could convince her libido that it was the right truth.

"Jackson, I have work to do and I don't play games during work. Besides, I might have to drive back to Austin to finish up some tag ends if my staff can't handle it."

With that announcement, she wheeled the mare around and headed in the direction of the house. She'd make it look like she was going home but then go find Andy. He had to learn he couldn't daddy her all the time. She had responsibilities.

She was disappointed that he didn't follow her, but she did have things to do. She chided herself. She needed to get her head back in the game and stop worrying about Jackson Knight. But oh, her core was tingling something awful.

She sent Andy a text and asked him where he was. About three minutes later he responded. *"Jackson said to tell you when you contacted me to go home."*

"I've just left from him. Where are you?"

"Heading towards the stables. Meet you there."

Piper was not going to be dictated to and if that is how Jackson Knight thought this was going to go, he was wrong, so incredibly wrong. And like anyone else in her world, she needed to be clear about her expectations.

"I think you got your man riled up, Miss Piper." He said as he began to walk towards the supply closet in the stables.

"He'll get over it. He always does." But she was worried just a tad. She was irritated more. She didn't have time to play this cat and mouse game with him.

Discussing the work and what was next needed, Piper held her tongue right before she told Andy about the core samples update. The fewer people who knew about the report, the better it was. She was good at keeping information to assist in the final deal.

In this case, until she knew why her Pops had gotten the sample and not explained it to anyone, not even Andy, she didn't know what he was thinking. Besides there was that Blackwell Company to keep an eye on so she changed conversations and settled on minimum cattle price.

"I understand that you usually do the buying and selling but I'm going to hire for a one-time contract someone who brokers cattle for a living. He is a professional middleman." Piper laughed. "Never thought I'd willingly bring in a middleman but I think we can do better on price. My research seems to bear that out.

While it'll cost some and we'll lose a portion of the extra profits to pay his contract fees, I think it's worth it to see what we can get. We can take it from there. Besides I need bison and he knows the best places to get them."

"Miss Piper, we've been selling our own herd for too many years to count. I don't like it. Why do you think this guy can do better?"

"Because he guarantees better or he charges us nothing."

"What? What type of crazy fool would do that?"

"The kind that is confident that he can produce. See you tomorrow. I'm on my way to Austin. Maybe you should invite Cody and the Knight brothers to dinner tomorrow night. I'll bring my projections and all of you might help me work on my thoughts on the amount to sell. Besides, I need Jackson to help with breeding guidance. Since it will be a working dinner I'll order from the café. Something hearty you boys will enjoy." She lifted her hand in salute as she held her phone to her ear and strode absently in the direction of the house.

The next afternoon she flagged Josie down.

"I finished the list you left and thought I would bake a cake for dessert tonight. I hope you don't mind."

"Mind? Are you kidding? I love you. I hope it's big because we have strapping men to feed."

Josie smiled. "I baked enough, even for those boys."

Piper sat and gave Josie a considering look while watching her file the new paperwork Piper had brought back.

"Josie, what would you say if I offered you a permanent position here at the ranch doing what you're doing now and more?"

"Well, I guess I'd want more details and would have to figure out what to do with the last three months of my apartment lease. And where would I stay? There aren't apartments nearby."

"Well, the company could either buy out your lease or pay your rent for the next three months, so you could transition slowly. I'd say you were welcome to do as you are and stay in the house here with me and Jackson. I'd also say there would be a pay increase because your responsibilities would be greater."

"Is it a real offer, Ms. Gentry?

"It is."

"Then I'd like to accept. I don't have anything holding me in Austin and this place kind of grows on you."

"Yes, I see that maybe the scenery is appealing as well. I sure think the Clear Knight Ranch has some tempting sights."

"Yes, ma'am. It does seem to." Her face was flushed and Piper decided she'd embarrassed the young woman enough. Piper went back to work.

"Ms. Gentry, I need to talk to you about something. It might be nothing but—"

"Sure, but first if you don't start calling me Piper, I'm going to quit answering. Of course, use Ms. Gentry when appropriate but with the group here and between us, please call me Piper."

Josie wiped her hands on her slacks and squared her shoulders. "Thank you, I will. So, Piper, I have a concern."

Piper leaned back in her father's desk chair that she'd now inherited and said, "Shoot."

Josie nodded and looked out of the open office door.

"Do you want to close the door, Josie?"

"If I could?"

Piper sat up straighter in her seat and indicated the door. "Then close it."

The heavy oak divider closed, and the room was quiet. The walls and heavy wooden doors effectively kept sound in the room it came from.

"I found Andy and another worker digging around in the office when I came down this morning. You'd left yesterday so Mr. Knight came in late and left early. I startled the men. They had no idea I was here. I asked what they needed, and could I help them. Andy mumbled something about making things difficult and they left quickly."

"I'll try to find out what they were looking for. Did they come back?"

"No and the funny thing is, I know I have never stayed behind when you go to Austin. I take any ranch work and go to the apartment or office, so that is the understanding. I don't think even Mr. Knight knew I was here."

"Why do you think that?"

"You know he always announces when he is retiring to bed and checks the security, then knocks on the door to see if I'm okay for the night?"

"Yes."

"He didn't. I was still awake, but it was late and normally it doesn't matter what time it is, he still checks."

"I bet you're right. So that didn't happen. Then this morning you found Andy and another worker looking where?"

"In the files and so I checked where they were looking, and it appears as though they were looking at those I have set on your desk."

Piper reached to the corner of the varnished top and picked them up. "What's in here?"

"There are private papers like the power of attorney that we signed when we were all together and other authorizations, the will, and things like that."

"It's odd that he would want to look in this file because he knows all of the information."

"The other paperwork was birth certificates and the like in the second file folder so I pulled it but didn't think he was really interested in that but who knows? I just wanted you to be informed."

"Yes, I needed to know. Thanks Josie. From now on, I think we will lock the office if I can find a key to it. If not, we'll have to put a new handle. And Josie, I'll tell Jackson but let's not announce it to anyone else. I trust Andy, but he did cross the line digging in the personal filing cabinet. He knows which filing cabinet is which. I think we lock the cabinets, too. I do know where those keys are. Can you handle that after I get things lined up? For tonight, we lock what we are able to."

"Yes, I'll handle it."

"Great. And Josie?"

"Yes?"

"Welcome to Gentry Ranch."

Chapter 11

Josie ran into town to purchase the new door lock and pick up dinner while Piper finished her GWI board presentation and some tweaking on the ranching paperwork. She felt more relaxed now that she had made the decision and acted on hiring Josie for the ranch only. It was going to make the separation of work and blending of time so much easier.

Her personal assistant, Leanne, had children so couldn't come but promised if this was a way of life, then she would bring the kids out on the weekends to give her a hand. It would be a win-win. The kids would love it.

But now it wouldn't be necessary, and she sent off an email to Leanne to let her know the Austin office was all hers but she would need a replacement for Josie on a permanent basis.

Leanne's response was, "It's about time."

Josie was single, no steady boyfriend, eager to learn, and she was bubbly when things were hard. And the girl liked to cook. What more could a boss want?

Running upstairs to take a quick shower, Piper was drying her hair when Jackson, wet from his own shower, tackled her to the bed.

She squealed and then started laughing.

"You're wet!"

"And now so are you." His eyebrows bounced up and down as she tried to push his cold dripping body away.

"We have some unfinished businesswoman." Jackson said in mock sternness.

"Jackson, please, I can't be worried about what you think all the time. There are days that I'm so busy I have to remember where I am. Please don't be as worried about me and can't you forget about yesterday?

Honestly, I'm sorry about the lack of communication. It was wrong of me. I'm used to a different system where I check on everyone else, but it is rare for anyone to do the same for me."

He kissed her gently as he ran his finger along her cheek and chin line. "I'm beginning to see that, baby cakes, however I'm a man of my word. I have to make good on my promise so roll over and let's get this over with." He patted her thigh.

Piper grunted her disagreement but rolled over.

"Oh, sweetness you are the most beautiful woman I have ever known. Honestly, could anyone have a more perfect ass?" He rubbed and massaged the pale flesh and landed two little, barely stinging swats on each cheek. "Are you going to text me when you go out alone? Before you leave?" He continued to knead her flesh.

"Yes, I promise to be better about it," was her breathy response. He popped both cheeks bringing them to a light flush creating a powerful hunger in her core.

"Good. Now that my obligation has been met," he leaned down and kissed both bottom cheeks. "I want to really show you what a spanking can be like." Rolling her over to her back, he stood and lifted both legs up in the air with one hand, exposing her damp, curly muff, the back of her thighs, and her bottom. He smiled when he heard her take a few shallow breaths. She was excited. His shaft was in agreement.

"Jackson, what are you doing?"

"Teaching you about spanking, baby. There is so much you don't know."

"I figured that out when I researched it."

"You researched? Why?" He held her thighs apart, leaned down between them to place his mouth on her breasts, to kiss and caress them with his tongue.

"Because you like it. Oh, Jackson, that is so good." She arched to give him more access. He chuckled.

He lifted his head. "Thank you, baby, but now you can be someone who writes the research."

He landed a swat on her bottom and rubbed the sting away. He did it several times and soon he could see her almost hold her breath for the next connection. Jackson pushed her further up on the bed when her wiggles were getting too excited. Pressing her knees against her chest, he splayed her legs open wide. Leaning down between them, he kissed her mons, lightly exhaling his heated breath across her skin before separating the puffy lips and breathing again. She shivered.

"Jackson, please."

"Daddy. We are alone, in the bedroom, and you are getting your ass spanked and your pussy played with. It's Daddy time."

"Please, Daddy?"

"Please what, sweetheart? Please stop, please kiss me, tongue me, suck me? What, sugar? What do you need?"

He held his face just above the juncture of her thighs and nudged her mons but nothing else. He loved her mews and wiggles trying to entice him to figure out her needs.

"Oh God, all of it, I need all of it."

He chuckled. "Why didn't you say so, although it sounds a bit greedy."

His tongue went deep diving and Piper tried to come off the bed. She held his head in place as though he might fly away and leave her wanting.

"Now, now, if you can't stay still, I'll have to tie you to the bed."

Piper was immediately still. "You do that too?"

He smiled. "I can. Why, do you like it or hate it?"

"I love it."

"Ah, I'll get the supplies later. But right now, we are finishing this, so we can have dinner. Our guests are waiting."

"What? I forgot. Jackson, we have to stop."

"No, I'm finishing my appetizer and you're allowing me to. Be still." His mouth descended on her again. "I have to start again."

"No, they'll hear." The slap was loud as it echoed, and he did it again.

"Daddy. I won't tell you again. If you want to come, you will mind me. And, baby girl?"

"Yes, Daddy?"

He smiled. "Don't make a sound." His tongue ran the entire strip of wet glistening pinkness.

"Oh, God." she whispered before she moaned. "So good."

"Shh. Daddy will have to spank you if you are loud and then everyone will know you were getting your ass beat."

Her eyes widened, and she held her breath. It was the most erotic thing he'd ever seen.

"That is so, so, sexy, Daddy."

Piper was sweating and panting but emitting no telling sound of his lovemaking and when she could handle it no longer, she exploded in brilliant orgasmic display. Twice. He didn't even try hard. She was so responsive.

He expected that when he had time to really play she would enjoy him taking control. She was so enticing. He allowed her to rest for a few minutes before kissing her hard on the lips and rolling off the bed to dress.

"Come on baby cakes, time for dinner." He rolled her over just enough to expose one luscious bottom cheek. He slapped it.

She squealed and made a noise of discontent. He smiled. This is how it all began, with a squeal and a groan. He couldn't wait for the screams.

ᐧᗊᐧ

The gate was going up today and while Andy was out on the ranch, Piper oversaw the process. She had her security system up and running the week before. Just as the gate was undergoing its final testing, two men with suits drove up to the workers and sat in their car for a few moments.

Piper, having been clued into the ways of breaches when her company was large enough to employ a security person, stopped the work.

"Excuse me. Will you stop all work and take a break? I don't want anyone to hijack the information you input for the scanners or the keyed entry so blank it and take a break."

"You got it. We'll move our truck over to block the gate and wait on you."

Piper made sure her Bluetooth was off and then she called Jackson. She needed a show of force and intent. She wanted Blackwell to stay away. The men sat in the vehicle a little longer before making motions to exit. Piper walked up to them.

"Hold on just a moment please. Jackson is on his way but until he gets here, I need to know your name and your intentions."

The man in the driver's seat spoke. "I'm Martin Lathrop. I represent Blackwell Investments. We are here to continue our discussion with Mr. Garth Gentry."

Jackson's big black truck pulled up next to the car, and he climbed out. Piper smiled. She was never so thankful for the largeness of that man until today.

"Hey, baby cakes." He kissed her quickly on the lips and put his arm around her.

"Jackson, this is Mr. Martin Lathrop, and he represents Blackwell Investments. He wants to talk to Pops. Funny thing is, his company knows Pops passed away, so what do you think is going on?"

"I think we will ask Mr. Lathrop." Both looked directly at the man who was turning an uncomfortable red.

"I'm sorry. I know it must be in the file, but I neglected to refresh my memory. I apologize and offer my condolences for your loss. I need to speak to the owner now."

"Oh, that'd be me then. Jackson and I make all the decisions together."

"But what happened to your brother, Rafe Gentry?"

"Wait, you could remember that you spoke to my brother and even recall his name but you couldn't remember my Pops had died? I don't think I will be able to trust your word, Mr. Lathrop. You need to leave my property."

"No, no, wait. I have a generous offer to make for your property."

"Oh, well then, make your offer. I already have two other offers as well, but I'll entertain yours."

"Two others?"

"Yep, Jackson here has first dibs, and then GWI has a bid option."

"What would GWI want with this property?"

"Oh, you know them? Same as you, I imagine. So why do you want it, exactly?"

"Luxury residential development."

"So, you have asked other landowners that are butting up next to our property then, as well?"

"Yes, ma'am and this is the property holding out. We need it to complete the project. Mr. Gentry had assured us that he would sell before, uh, his demise."

"Really? I wonder why he never mentioned it to us. Well anyway, what is your offer, exactly?"

Lathrop reached to the console between him and the man who had yet to speak, pulling out a bright yellow envelope. He wordlessly passed it to her. Piper accepted the envelope.

"Is contact information inside with the offer?" She knew it was, but she decided to continue her act of intelligence but cluelessness as far as acquisitions went.

He nodded.

"Thank you for dropping by. I'll take a look and see if it's in the running."

"I am authorized to say that there is a small amount of negotiation room, should that help you decide."

"Yes, well, thanks again." Jackson took Piper's hand and walked her away from the vehicle as it was backed up and driven away.

"You were naughty, Piper Gentry."

"Nope, I was being careful not to tip our hand as we work through this mess. I was being a shrewd businesswoman. Did you hear how many lies that man was caught in? And he still had no problem leaving us an offer like that was the way business was conducted every day." Piper's indignation was getting the better of her.

"Simmer down, Pips, I hear the anger, but you need to keep your temper even after they've left." Jackson looked over at the workers. "Can they get back to work now?"

Piper looked over at the men and waved at them. "Hey, thanks for taking that break. Go ahead and finish your testing. I appreciate it."

"You want me to keep an eye on them while you open the offer?"

"No but if you have a few minutes, I'd like to look at it with you."

"Sure. I'm kind of curious." He leaned back on his pickup.

Piper opened the envelope. "Wow, that's a lot of zeros." She showed the paper to Jackson.

"Yep, seven point five million dollars is not peanuts. Five thousand an acre is what it comes down to or close. Not sure if that includes equipment, as is, or what but land isn't that expensive here. There's no doubt something is going on."

"Yep and I'm going to find out what."

Before Piper drove into Austin she went through the list of things to accomplish and how they were coming. Josie pulled out her tablet, ready to add or subtract from the running list she kept.

"Okay, we have the building security lights up, cameras in place, new locks on the office and equipment, so take those off the list. Office equipment updated and all in working order, so that's done."

Jose nodded and looked up at Piper. "We need to take inventory. If I'm working in this office and cooking in that kitchen, I need supplies. And can we get someone around to do a little light housekeeping?"

"Yes, can you take care of that?"

"I know someone who could come by once or twice a week and do the basics. She is the house helper over at the Clear Knight since their housekeeper cooks for the hands too. She works all day Monday and Friday and half days on Wednesdays, so she could fit us in Tuesday and Thursday."

"Will we need her both days? I think we would be good with either day, but you will have to monitor things because I'll be in Austin."

"No problem. Now what about meat? The freezer is pretty bare."

"Oh, I have something on that, let me pull it out... yes, here is the information for the packers. They usually sell pork and chicken but for fish, you'll have to send someone fishing. For beef, talk to Jackson about getting a cow slaughtered. The packers will pick it up and take it from there. I want the ear tag so I can take it off the inventory. And that reminds me, we need to do a ranch wide stock inventory as well. If we are about to bring in more cattle, we need to know the numbers just prior to delivery."

"I'll charge the scanner. Should I just tell Andy to do it?"

"No, I want to do the inventory. We are adding different stock and we have to look at size for grazing needs. This isn't so different from finance except I have to leave the office to do it. I'm calling a cattleman I met in Denver. He lives in Wyoming but he raises Beefalo, cattle and buffalo. He offered to help anyone that had a thought towards beefalo or buffalo."

"I've never heard of beefalo but sounds like it's a buffalo cow."

"Yep. I hear they are good eating and of course I'll need to run this by Jackson. He might know about breeding them. Anyway, I have the last livestock numbers and I want to do it so I know the numbers are right. Can you see if Jackson has any time to help in the next week or two?"

Josie sighed. "No disrespect but he's just going to ask to talk to you."

"I'm up to my eyeballs in work so he will have to talk to you. If he pushes back, tell him I'm to the make an appointment or take a number, stage."

Josie laughed and Piper didn't push the point but she was absolutely serious. Piper had been experiencing a short temper for days. She wondered if it had to do with her work schedule, the offer, or her lack of good sleep. Add in her hormones for a dessert topping and staying clear of her was a wise mood.

Jackson had been working late so he came in for dinner and went back out only to take her to bed when he finally dragged in. The next morning it was a toss-up who was out of bed faster. She was hoping things would calm down soon.

Every day since she had accepted that envelope at the end of last week, she had fielded a call from Mr. Lathrop asking if she had come to a decision on the offer. She chatted, clarified what it covered and then finally, she had to say she didn't have any answer yet.

"I'm sorry, Mr. Lathrop. My siblings are out of the country and while I have access to one, the other is not easy to locate while on assignment. I have a call out to him. That is the best I can do right now. Why don't I call you when I speak to him?" He said he would call again.

Piper had other things to worry about. She had proven to the lab that she was who she said she was and while they were still going to mail the results to the ranch at the end of the week, she could pick up a copy today. She was on her way this morning.

As she drove, she thought of Jackson. He did everything he promised he'd do and more. He never left her to work out something he knew how to do and he gave her a wide berth if it was her expertise. He calmly listened to her as she explained the financial gains they were making and offered his opinion when it came to next strategies.

And Piper loved him more than she could quantify on paper or in her mind. Without Jackson, she would be more of a wreck than she currently was, and that was saying something significant. But unless they made a concerted effort to connect, they wouldn't see each other except dinner and bedtime.

She had to leave him a note to remind him of the Austin trip and that she would return on Friday. Thursday night she had a dinner meeting. She didn't mention the core samples to anyone, even avoiding re-mentioning them to Jackson. She hadn't even discussed it with Josie except she'd seen a cryptic note in the planner. Thankfully, Andy had not inquired about them. She pulled in the lab's parking lot and walked inside.

When the person she had been dealing with came out to meet her, she smiled. "I'm anxious to see the results but I'm not sure I will understand them. Do you have time to do some explaining and educating?"

"Absolutely, let me print them off for you."

By the time she left the lab, she knew that there were several minerals that were profitable on the property if they came in large enough quantities but one of the most profitable, because it was the easiest acceptable, was the crude oil deposits. One core sample even detected some flecks of gold but mostly there were a variety of quartz, topaz, and possibly opals in the ground. She only thought of opals in Australia.

Oil. That is what this was all about? Oil? There must be a vein or an expectation of a quantity trapped in there for Blackwell to want it so badly. Piper understood it was a crap shoot until they actually tried to tap it but there was enough expectation that she needed to be careful. She called her attorney from the office and then she called Jackson. Rashid would call Blackwell Investments and decline on her behalf, but Piper was worried about the fallout.

"Don't say you are with GWI. I don't want him to think I sold to us."

"No problem. But I am going to file these papers so they are recorded before I call and decline their offer."

"Sounds good to me, I'm just following your lead." The laughter on the other end of the line was real.

"Whatever you tell yourself to make you feel less like a barracuda."

She chuckled. "Thanks, point taken. I hope your call stops their calls."

"It should."

The next morning, just before lunch, Blackwell Investments was informed that their offer was declined and that there would be no renegotiations. The Clearwater Incorporated dba Gentry Ranch was not on the market.

She hadn't told Jackson she was incorporating based on her paperwork and those mineral samples because she hadn't been home yet. She hoped he wasn't too upset.

Late that afternoon, her cell phone rang. It was Josie.

Chapter 12

The person on the other end of the call was panting and her voice trembled as though running and scared. "Hey Josie, what's going on? What's wrong?"

Josie was nearly frantic and her words were tumbling out over themselves. "Shot. One of your workers has been shot, Piper."

"Shot? Josie, what's going on there? Where is Andy? Jackson?"

Josie was saying something, but it seemed as though she were speaking to someone else, the voice distant and indistinct. She came back on.

"Piper? The EMTs are here. I'm outside at the gate, but Walker isn't going to let me stay here. Jackson is riding with the ambulance and Sawyer is over at the corral with Andy waiting for them."

Josie's voice became distant again. She was speaking to someone, likely Walker. Then Piper heard something that would have made her laugh if she wasn't so worried.

"I'm going inside. Did you just slap my ass? Who does that? All right, I'm going. Piper? I have to go back inside. You can call me if you have more questions, but Jackson will give you a call as soon as he has more complete information, and he said not to worry, it was more of a flesh wound."

The phone went dead. Piper tried Jackson's cell but it went to voice mail. There was a shooting? Someone was shot on the ranch? Did the poachers come back for more than the four-legged beasts? Piper called Rashid and filled him in on the historic information she and the research department uncovered and then she filled him in on the current happenings.

"How's your security?"

"I forgot. We just put a system in that includes cameras. I'm going to access the cameras. You're brilliant."

"Glad I could help. Piper. It could be an accident, so don't jump to conclusions. Let me know when you get more information. Unfortunately, even if it is a shooter, unless you can identify him or her, there is little if anything that can be done about this. You need to know that up front. I know it isn't what you want to hear but the law is pretty clear on this and even you have to accept some things."

"What you're trying to tell me is that I can't go after Blackwell simply because I think the timing of this is too perfect for a coincidence."

"Precisely."

"We'll see what the camera shows." Before she could look at the video, she was fielding another call, this time from Leanne, her assistant.

"Some men were here looking for you from Blackwell Associates. I informed them that you would be back late this afternoon if your meetings didn't run long. They wouldn't leave a message, but one man wrote on the back of the business card they left, it says, 'The wise choice.' What does it mean?"

"I wish I knew. I'll be in shortly." Piper knew exactly what it meant but the wording was clever. It could easily mean choosing them as a company not as a procurer of your off-the-market property that now had increased in value.

She pulled up the app on her tablet and watched the scene as it was unfolding at the ranch. The hand wasn't one she had dealt with much, but he was a good worker as far as she could tell and had been at the ranch a couple of years. She wondered if he would be back after this. Her phone rang. Jackson.

"Hey Jackson, what's going on there? I have the camera up and was about to go through the video from lunch through the incident."

"Good idea but Sawyer, Walker and I will handle this. I know you hired Josie because she is competent, but this shook her up."

"How can I help her?"

"Nothing extra, I think Walker has her covered." Piper thought back to the end of her conversation with Josie and figured he was right. "Everyone else okay? No one else hurt?"

"Everyone else is safe but I'm concerned about how someone could have gotten close enough to the paddocks to shoot your man. I mean, the gate is still closed. There are buildings surrounding the area they were in before the shooting and actually it was two shots, one missed, one hit. Andy was close by but not in the paddock with them."

"I have cued up the camera. I'll watch and call you back. Is the sheriff gone?"

"Yep, they're all gone. We're going to walk the fence to see if we can get an understanding of where they got in or where they were standing. It would help if you could look for where the shot came from and who was around him when it happened. I have to tell you, I think something is off on this but I don't have a clue what. Yet."

"I'll pack up and come home."

"You will not. Do your work there. We have this covered and I'll call you later, at your desk, where I know you'll be safe."

She thought about the business card in front of her and wondered how safe Jackson would think she was if he knew about it. "You do know I can forward the call to my cell, right?"

"I do, and you know what will happen if you do that or come home before Friday morning, right?"

"I have had just about enough of the bossiness. I'll finish what I need to do, then I'll come home and if that is before Thursday you'll have to deal with it."

"Yes, I will. Expect your ass to be a variety of shades of red."

She could almost taste the angry resentment before she swallowed it down again. That man could be infuriating, and her body was supposed to be in unity with her brain. It clearly was on the other end of the spectrum. She grimaced. Maybe love and hate were indeed closely related extreme emotions.

"I'll call after I review the feed."

She hung up before he could respond. This was one of the days she reconsidered keeping her office in Austin. She really needed to just call it and keep her main satellite office on the ranch. Jackson might have something to say about it but if she could work it out, she would sell her condo and move her office. Maybe she should feel out the board on that move.

She only occasionally saw people who weren't her staff and she could video chat or conference easily if she upgraded their software. Leanne could run her portion in Austin and be the face of the office if need be. It would put more pressure on the newly divorced mother of two, but Leanne needed the money and her mother kept the kids so she could work.

If Piper moved her office, they could set standard meetings for one day of the week and Piper would just stay overnight in a hotel. Much more economical and less stressful than what she was doing now. Jackson couldn't be upset about that unless he didn't want her around during the week. No, that's stupid. If he hadn't been there today things would have been much worse. She wondered why Andy didn't call her. He probably knew Jackson and Josie were already on it. She turned on the recording.

Piper clicked off the feed and sat back in her chair. It was after seven and her staff had left hours ago. Except for security and housekeeping, her offices were closed. Normally she loved the empty office but the quiet, after the events of the day, was unsettling. She tried to call Jackson, but it just rang. It was too late to be out on the ranch, but he could be in the barns working and couldn't hear his phone. She called Josie.

"Hey, Josie, how are you after today?"

"Good. I'm fine now. Sorry I was a little keyed up about the whole thing. I just couldn't believe it'd happened."

"I know, none of us could and I've reviewed the recording. There isn't anything that I could see really. It had to be a long-range rifle with an expensive scope. I looked at every person I could, and no one had a gun and I looked at the direction it came from but couldn't see a thing."

"The Knights are pretty intense right now trying to check access routes and all. Did Andy call you about the fences or did Jackson tell you about the mixed cattle?"

Piper had heard about all she could handle for one

excruciatingly long day. "No," she sighed, "what about them?"

"I'm not supposed to say but Andy said a section of fence had been cut and evidently it happened this week. Jackson found some of your cattle in with his and vice versa."

"Why were you supposed to keep quiet about it and who wanted you to?"

"Jackson. Because he was taking care of it, I guess. I hope I don't get in trouble over this."

"Don't you worry, my girl. I hired you to be my eyes and ears as well as office assistant. No one is going to be upset with you unless they expect me to come and rain on their parade."

"I hope you're right, but could you maybe get the information out of Jackson yourself?"

"Yes, but this is ridiculous." Piper heard mumbling in the background. Male voices were talking to her.

"Well, it's too late anyway, the Knights are here." Piper thought she heard a deep male voice, and something sounded like a chastisement then a kiss.

"Jackson, I'm getting your dessert, here, talk to Piper. Good night, Piper."

Jackson? What was he doing kissing Josie when she was Walker's main squeeze? Is that why he didn't want her coming home too soon? Josie was sweet on Walker, wasn't she? No, Jackson claimed to love Piper. She was just tired. *Stop being a teenage drama queen.* The question wouldn't quite leave her mind, though.

"Piper, are you resting, working, or driving?"

"I'm taking a break. I have a couple of meetings tomorrow and then I'm coming back."

"You don't need to. I can handle things here, honey. You should finish your business so that when you're here, you aren't so stressed and can be fully present."

"Sure, I do and there isn't anything else I can't handle from the ranch right now. I'll be present enough unless you don't want me there for some reason."

"Of course, I want you here, every day would be perfect. We'll get there soon. Look baby cakes, it's been a long day. I need to shower and go to bed. I'll see you tomorrow night then, yeah?"

"Yeah, sure. I should go home too."

"Wait. You aren't calling me from home?" The change in tone was classic Jackson in protective mode.

"Nope, still at the office but I was thinking of going home right after I finish my review of this last project."

"Go home. Finish it at home."

"I'm almost done."

"What does *almost done* look like, half an hour, hour, what?"

She was feeling the familiar twinge in her pink bits. Great, now she was aching for the man.

"Jackson, I have to go." Who had flipped the crazy switch? Mineral deposits, shootings, damaged property, and lost cattle were going on at her ranch, her boyfriend was kissing her assistant and now she had the hots for him because he had put on the dominant hat. And to top it off, Blackwell seemed to not want to take 'No thank you' as a viable response to his offer.

"I'm calling you in one hour. If you're not at home by then, expect a hot—"

"I'm cleaning up right now and when I get back to the ranch, I expect your hot ass in my bed. Bye." She hung up on his deep chuckle of amusement.

Jackson was out working when she drove up to the ranch gate. Before he returned for supper, she got a call and was pinned in the office all through the meal trying to avoid a crisis with one of her projects. Jackson had left her alone other than to come in and bring her plate. As she was in the middle of another call he came in to kiss her goodnight and look pointedly at the clock on her desk. In one eventful day, her whole organized schedule had gone to hell in the proverbial hand basket and she hated feeling out of complete control.

At eleven she took a shower and fell into bed next to a snoring Jackson. He seemed to know, even in his sleep, that she was there. He turned to his side snaking his right arm around her middle and pulling her into him. She fell straight to sleep snuggled into the warm, clean and spicy scent of Jackson Knight.

Piper awoke to the aroma of coffee, bacon and buttery syrup floating past her nose. She grinned and stretched. "Wake up, baby cakes. You'll be late for work."

"I'm the boss, I can't be late," she said completing her stretching with a satisfied hum.

"Is that right? Well you're in the wrong room to be boss."

"What's that supposed to mean?"

"In this room, I'm boss."

"I see, so come over here and show me how bossy you can be in this room."

"That, my naughty girl, is called topping from the bottom or driving from the passenger seat, or..."

She threw her pillow in Jackson's direction. "Okay, I get it."

"Oh," the door closed firmly, "you're going to get it, all right." He stripped before her hungry eyes and dove for the bed. It bounced as a way of announcing his arrival. Snatching her around the waist, her "hey" floated in the breeze as her breasts squished against his chest.

"You have been naughty, Piper Gentry, and we have to get that out of the way first." He rolled her over in a flash.

"Jackson, you've been naughty too. You kissed my assistant."

"I most certainly did not," he said compressing her bottom cheek with his burning slap.

"I heard you," she said, rubbing her offended part. Another stinging swat and she was rubbing the other side.

"You couldn't have because it never happened." Four quick swats bringing more tingling forced a grunt from her.

"Yes, while we were on the phone last night. Stop it."

"Last ones." He played her bottom like it was a bongo set then rolled her over to lie on her warmed, achy flesh.

"That wasn't me."

He placed his full weight on her and took her lips in an intense melding. The combination of weight and deep, probing kiss had Piper creaming. "It was Walker."

"But you were there."

"Yep, and Sawyer but if you don't hush up, I'm going to work before finishing this off."

"No, I'm sorry. Come inside, please, Jackson. I don't need anything but you inside me."

She knew her desperation was clear. She wasn't lying, she needed him to be part of her. She loved the erotic touch of his fingers in her nectar as it flowed from her core. She mewed her need as he smeared her essence around her delicate area, moving his fingers in and out a few times.

"You are good for my ego. You're always so ready for me," he told her.

She felt the walls of her inner sanctum stretch, her muscles singing in excitement as he slid inside, his cock fully immersed. The gentle expansion set the tingling off throughout her core. With just a little angling he had spread her wide, settled in her harbor and was rubbing her clit continually as he bobbed in and out of her. She slipped her hand down between them to caress his ball sac and he pumped faster.

Now it was his turn to moan his pleasure. "You are so hot, sweetheart." He tweaked her nipple and stared into her eyes as her whole being tensed. She lifted her bum up, pushing herself onto his shaft allowing the first waves of sensation to wash over her. Jackson waited, keeping up his rhythm steady but slower. When she began to relax, he lifted up to kiss her lips, moving down to suckle her breasts, giving each special attention.

"Shh, no sound now, Pips, nothing."

Piper widened her eyes, and she imagined her pupils dilated because that was one thing that immediately went straight to her clit. If she had to be silent, the room suddenly became too hot to handle. Jackson took control in every way then, thrusting until she crested again, signaling him to let go. He did, allowing his own pleasure to wash over him in hard crashing waves of release.

She smiled, they had always been good sexually and if possible, they were only getting better.

Chapter 13

As she stepped out of the shower the aroma of a hearty breakfast tantalized her nose and tickled her belly. She hurried to dress, hoping she could get a little before Jackson ate it all. It amazed her how much the man could eat. As she stepped into the dining room she was met by a group of men, devouring breakfast.

"Wow, is this a gathering of the chiefs or what?"

Piper looked around at all three Knight brothers, both ranch managers, and Josie digging into full plates. "To what do we owe this honor?"

She sat down in the only empty seat next to Jackson and snagged a piece of bacon from his plate.

"Hey now, I might love you but taking a man's bacon is pushing the limits of affection just a bit too far." Piper grinned as she crunched away.

Turning to fill her plate she asked, "So what brings you all here today? I didn't know we were having a meeting."

Jackson popped one of her potatoes O'Brien in his mouth before speaking. "I did, actually. We need to figure a few things out after yesterday."

"I agree. So, what are your thoughts?"

Piper sat eating her breakfast as the men laid out their concerns. She swallowed her bite.

"Okay, so as I see it, our security is really as good as it's going to get. No matter what we do, we can't stop bullets and still run cattle."

Andy shook his head. "The bigger problem is that the fences are being cut and the cattle are somehow crossing pastures from ours to Knight's land."

"I agree that it is a problem, one I wasn't made aware of." Piper sent Jackson and then Andy her best a chastising stare "But less enormous than someone shooting at us. Did our cowboy go home until he gets well?"

Andy nodded. "Yessum, we sent him home from the hospital."

"Good. Josie, make sure his pay is not changed and if he doesn't have any insurance, it was on the job, so we pay for whatever isn't covered."

Josie nodded. "Us and workman's comp, you mean."

"I'm sure he filed at the hospital. I don't even know if that is covered. But he pays nothing."

"Got it."

"Good, now about the mingling of cattle. We both chip and tag so there shouldn't be any problems. Who was going to tell me that we had this problem and just how long have we had it?"

Piper had taken on the CEO stance and was gratified when the others acknowledged it and allowed her to take the lead. She wondered the cost it was taking for the Knights to let her handle it. Her respect for the brothers went up another notch.

"We need a current inventory so Josie, get the chip reader ready this morning and we read until we find them all. Any we find not ours, we return home."

"Now, Piper, we don't have that kind of time," complained Andy.

"Why? The way I see it, we don't have any other choice. We don't have the luxury of ignoring the loss of cattle and neither, I bet, does anyone else."

"I have things I need to do without adding this to the list," grumbled Andy.

"Tell me. Maybe we can consolidate the efforts."

"There are fences and tack to mend, as well as the stables need some maintenance for starters."

Piper didn't know why there was such hostility in the mulish way that Andy was acting today but she intended to nip it in the bud.

"Okay, so we have seven hands working, right? Oops, six at the moment. So, two can ride the fences and—"

"That won't be enough to get the job done quickly, like it will need to be this time." Sawyer pushed his plate back and crossed his arms as though he were ready to defend his opinion. Piper changed her tact because it was obvious that the men in this room thought she was going to shoot down their every word.

"All right, so how many men would be good, Sawyer?"

"Probably four could handle it but six would be much better. The pressing need is the perimeter lines. The interior ones can be handled a tad bit slower. Just put your bulls far enough from each other, but I would definitely keep them on the interior fenced areas because you don't want to put them at risk of mixing. Jackson here would have a hissy fit if they got in with the breeding stock."

She glanced over at Jackson and saw his grim expression but to his credit, no words were spoken. He seemed content for now to let her go on. Piper knew how much Jackson's breeding stock was worth and how protective he was of them. He had to be. She needed to protect them as well.

"Okay, so how about this. We hire some temp ranch hands. I'll call out to the barber shop and see if there are any on the hiring board we could tap into. Besides, he'll know who else is looking or willing to hire out."

"But that will take time—time we don't have."

"Look, Andy, I appreciate this has put a big paw in your pie so to speak but we can't just throw the shovel in the ditch when we hit rock. We need to find another place to dig our hole."

Andy remained quiet, but Cody spoke. "I could probably offer two guys."

"Nope, I am not taking from you unless we are desperate. hold on."

She looked a moment and then hit some buttons and held the phone to her ear. "Roger? Hey, this is Piper Gentry. Good. Well, thank you. Roger, we need a few more men to work temp for a bit, anyone worth calling on your wall?" She looked at the men who seemed stymied that she called while everyone was still discussing things. They didn't know Piper on a mission, but they were becoming acquainted with her.

"The Kirkland boys?" She looked up at the men around her seeing approval in the nodding heads.

"How many are they? Four? Oh my. And they're all looking for work? Oh, I'm sorry to hear that. Can you hold on just a sec? Thanks." She hit mute. "Okay, Kirkland boys. Their dad has gotten too sick to keep the majority of their place going.

The younger two boys, seventeen and eighteen are keeping up with things there fine, but the others need work. What do you say?"

"I'd say that's a perfect solution. No training needed there." Walker was pleased.

She unmuted the phone. "Roger? Can you give me their number? Okay, I'll hold." She spoke to the room. "They had just asked about work not five minutes ago. He thinks they're next door."

"Hello? Jason? Hey, this is Piper Gentry."

They had four new hires who would be out after they grabbed their gear and told their family. They would stay at the bunkhouse for a week and then see how things were. The rest of the objections were laid to rest, and they kicked around some other ideas for a bit before Piper spoke again.

"Okay, I'm moving my personal satellite office to the ranch in a couple of weeks, the first of next month for sure."

Andy stood up quickly and went to get coffee, but Piper wasn't sure he didn't use that as a cover for his irritation. The rest seemed okay with it except Jackson.

"We need to discuss this," was his cryptic response.

"We will but I've made up my mind and polled the board. They agree it will be fine. If things work as I expect, I'll make it permanent and hire or promote a second vice president."

"Um, Piper?" asked Josie. She looked over at Walker who had said less than his brothers today.

"Yep." Piper redirected herself to give Josie her full attention.

"Um, well... I'm... um..."

Walker's quietly solid voice cut Josie off. "Piper, does Josie's job require that she live at the ranch?"

"Oh. Well, kind of. I mean, she can't go back to Austin to live, obviously, but if there is a close place she wants to go at night, like ten miles or so, then that would work. Why? Do you have a place you want to rent Josie?"

"No, I thought, well Walker and I thought—"

"Josie is coming over to the Clear Knight to stay with me. She'll work here but at night, she'd come home to me."

"Josie, that's fine. I don't want to command your whole life. I'm not an ogre." Piper smiled. "Usually."

"Thank you, Piper."

The tension fell from the room and Piper slapped the table as she stood. "Of course. I think our new house help is at the door, Josie. Now let's get to work and thanks guys for having my back in this. I appreciate that you all took time out of your busy day to help me figure things out. I'll get it right." Jackson grinned and shook his head as she appreciated their assistance. That man knew her too well. He didn't need his ego stroked but stood back as she fawned over the others.

His voice was liquid heat as he came up to hug her to him. "I'll be gone late tonight but I want you to be ready to tell me about this office move. I'm not sure I want you here when there is obviously going to be more dust kicked up."

"You mean guns fired?"

"Yes, maybe more than that."

"Then do you think something happened to Pops because he refused to sell like I just legally did?"

"We'll talk about it when I get home but until then, you do not go anywhere alone. That is not a sweet little reminder to be safe it is a thunderous demand that you better listen to and heed unless a blazing ass is what you really want."

"Jackson, I know what to do to stay safe and my whole day is filled with things that I have to do with Josie, so we will be together. That has to be enough."

He kissed her hard. "I don't want to go to jail for murder because someone decided driving through the barrier was better than finding a way around it or go another direction both physically and figuratively speaking."

"I understand. I'll be careful because I don't want to get hurt either. But you killing for me might be a turn on. Oh, wait, I don't want to visit you in federal prison, so I guess not."

Smack.

"Ouch, Jackson, that hurt."

"Remember that."

He took one last kiss before they went their separate ways for the day. The humming in her heart spread.

~

Jackson could feel the tension ratchet up for every day that nothing happened. They had returned each other's cattle and there were none missing. Summer's end was around the corner and being the last full hot month, tempers were flaring at the end of the day. Jackson was gingerly pulling his tired body out of the truck outside of the Gentry place when Josie exited, slamming the door behind her.

"Whoa there, girl, what are you so upset over?"

Jackson had gotten a chance to know Josie better, and he really liked her. If Walker stayed on this track, he could see them as a couple who eventually married. Josie was a city girl but she had adjusted well to the ranch life. Today, however, she was fuming.

"What? Oh," she hesitated. "Sorry but ever since she moved her working office here and is not in the GWI offices part of the week, she has worked more hours, worked harder, gotten snappier and expects me to do all the pick-up work. I mean, I know my job, but it has a start and end time and so does hers. Well, in theory that is."

"What're you talking about?"

"I mean, she gets an enormous amount of work done but have you noticed when she goes to bed?"

"With me, most days and we get up about the same time."

"I'd check on that because I promise you that there are log in times much earlier and later than I am positive you go to bed or get up."

"I see. What else?" He leaned back on his pickup as Josie continued to pour out her concerns and frustrations.

"Okay, don't get me wrong, because I love her like a sister, but she is a bitch these days. Not eating much either."

"The moodiness I understand. We've had a few conversations over that recently." For Josie, the implication was clear. She shivered. Jackson smothered his grin. He knew Walker and Josie had had a few of that caliber of conversation as well. "Why do you think she isn't eating?"

"I know she isn't because she passes on most lunches, bows out of more than toast or an orange for breakfast, and there is way too much dinner left for three adults to be eating it."

"But the ranch is running like clockwork."

"Yes, but at what cost and who is paying that bill?"

Jackson stood and thought back over their last days. Since the shooting she'd been a woman with a mission, that was true, but she did go to bed with him and was just getting out of the shower when he got up. But she was bowing out of sex these last days, saying she was too tired. He had been tired as well so cuddling sustained them.

"I'll handle it."

"Good, that's what Walker said. Something about time to take her in hand but said if I told you, things would get better."

"He was right. I'll figure things out."

"Oh, one more thing you should know. She blogs now."

"She does what now?"

"Blogs, you know a journal online for others to read."

"Right, I remember those, so what does she blog about?"

"The ranch mostly, learning it, the obstacles and so much more. You should look it up. Gentryranch.com. She's doing a good job, but she doesn't need another thing to do, you know?"

"Got it."

"I left dinner for you all. Andy isn't eating with you because he says it's lonely having meals at the house. He's eating with the guys. I cooked a favorite dish, enchiladas. See that Piper eats. She hasn't all day."

"Yep, leave it to me."

Josie jumped into Walker's pick-up leaning in for a kiss. Jackson was glad Walker found a sensible but fun woman. His brother had a great head for ranching but tended to be a little reckless in his dating choices, picking those women who only wanted to hook up. Not as bad as Sawyer, but commitment was never on the table, until now. Jackson waved them off and walked into the house.

"Piper, I'm home," he called. No answer.

He tossed his hat on the entry table and sat on the bench to take off his boots. "Piper!"

No response. He looked into the kitchen and front room but no Piper. He checked as he walked through the house finally reaching the office. She was sitting in her chair, intently working on something. He shook his head.

"Hey, Piper, what are you doing?"

"Working. Don't you have something to do?"

"I do but it's dinnertime and I need nourishment and kisses."

"Uh-uh, I'm not hungry."

"Yeah, well you need to eat so take a break. We're talking."

"I can't right now," she said never raising her head.

"Up now, stretch, get some food inside and relax a little."

"No, I'm busy. I'll get to it in a bit."

He touched her shoulder, and she jumped up from the chair. It rolled back, and she weaved, reaching for something to make purchase on to steady herself.

Jackson reached out to steady her and said, "Whoa, baby cakes, what's wrong?"

"Nothing, I got up too fast." Piper's voice was wobbly and her legs gave way.

Jackson swung her up in his arms and walked out of the room.

"No, Jackson."

He spoke as her body softly bounced on his chest, the rumbling of his deep voice resounded. "Hush now, baby. Daddy's in control."

Chapter 14

"Jackson, stop. Put me down. I have things to do."

He kept walking. Piper tried to wiggle, and the slap on her exposed leg resounded as he gave her his don't-be-naughty look.

"I'm not playing around here. I'm serious," said Piper.

She jerked in his arms, but he only tightened his hold on her. He gave her an incredulous look.

"And you, somewhere in your overtaxed mind, believe I'm playing? That I'm not serious? Baby cakes, Daddy is so very serious here."

Piper knew he wasn't messing around and she couldn't lie to his face but dammit, she wanted down and to finish what she was doing. He just didn't understand.

She tried a new tact. "Daddy, please, it won't take long.

Walking into the kitchen, the aroma slammed into her senses and ignited her taste buds causing her tummy to rumble and roar.

Gosh, maybe I am hungry.

"Piper Kay, be honest with Daddy. Did you eat breakfast?"

Piper scrunched her brows in deep contemplation. "Proba-bly."

"What?"

"What? Um," she looked around the kitchen, "egg and toast."

"Hm, how about an orange?"

"Did I?" she shrugged.

"What about lunch?"

"Okay, so maybe I missed lunch. Dinner smells amazing. Can I get down now? Please? Daddy?"

"I know what you are trying to do, calling me Daddy because you know I like it. Are you still dizzy?"

She read the concern in his face and heard it in his tone. She opened her mouth, but the words of denial wouldn't come out. "I think I'm good."

Kissing her lips lightly he placed her on the floor. She loved how he held her steady until she was sure she was indeed steady on her feet.

"Now, have a seat at the table and I'll dish us up a plate. I'm starving."

Piper turned to comply and felt a slight vertigo.

"That isn't a request, Pips, and I don't intend to repeat myself."

"I'm trying. I'm just a little woozy. It's nice to be waited on. Thank you." She sat in the chair Jackson pulled out.

"What to drink?"

"Is there wine?"

"I'm sure there is but not for you tonight. You need something that won't add to your light headedness or your instability."

"That's ridiculous."

"Nope, that's reality. Now tell me what you want or you get milk."

"Milk? Oh, actually with chocolate, that sounds really good. I think we have some in the cabinet over the coffee maker."

As they began to eat, neither spoke for the initial few moments before Jackson took a long drink of iced tea and asked, "So, what's going on? Why are you burning the candle at both ends?"

"Why do you think I am?"

She could hear his voice was purposefully well-modulated, and his control was contrived. She could imagine his need to make his displeasure known was strong, but he appeared almost casual. Piper hated that he used her own techniques on her.

"Piper, do you deny that you have gotten up on numerous occasions after I've gone to sleep, before I've woken up, or both to work on the ranch and your investment firm?"

"Not numerous times, Jackson. I've done it a few times, that's all."

"Quantify it please."

"What? Quantify it? Like say exactly how many times?"

"Yes, how any times."

He took a bite of his dinner as she put down her fork.

"I'm not a teenager."

He continued to chew and watch her, waiting for a response to his question.

"I don't know Jackson, a couple maybe."

She watched as he put his knife and fork on the table purposely. Some alarm went off in Piper's brain that said she had stepped well over his line of tolerance. What that actually meant for her was not fully understood until he scraped his chair back, stood and nearly yanked her out of her own seat.

For a large man who worked a hard physically demanding job all day, he moved with surprising agility as he put his stocking covered foot on her vacant chair then bent her over his waiting thigh, yanked down her yoga pants, and laid his hand on her backside. What was even more pronounced was his pounding of her now well exposed ass with his paddle-like hand.

After a number of hard fast swats on her fleshy mounds that sizzled her rear and brought tears to her tired eyes, he paused with his hand on her bottom. Her breath came with difficulty. She reached around to soothe her offended parts and Jackson slapped her hand away.

"So twice you left our bed to work in the middle of the night. Twice."

"Jackson."

Another round of air assaults landed on her bottom more intensely than the first. Piper screeched her dismay, kicking wildly then stopping as her precarious position was made known to her. She quickly caught the back of the chair with one hand and his calf with the other, trying to climb up his leg to get off his tree trunk thigh.

"Settle down, Pips." He waited until she had calmed and then asked, "Did you do it today? Yesterday?"

"Yes."

"More?"

She hesitated too long to answer, and he swatted her twice, once per thigh.

"Ow, stop. Okay, okay. I've done it a lot lately. I need to stay ahead, Jackson."

"Baby, we have to figure this out. I'm through with you doing too much." He rubbed her warm cheeks as he talked to her about how much he loved her. He stood her upright and kissed her lips before steering her back in the chair and returning to his.

"You need to eat more, honey."

Piper shifted in her seat, picking at her food even though she was still hungry. She didn't dare look at Jackson. She wanted to be angry with him not only for the "flash spanking" but she knew where he was going with this conversation.

She was furious to be called on the carpet for meeting her responsibilities and devastated that she was having difficulty harnessing her tears. *Or am I so tired from over doing it I can't keep my emotions in check?* Which she knew was closer to the truth.

Normally, people didn't ask her how she was doing except as a courtesy. They never listened to her answer assuming they even waited for a response. Jackson was not like that. He cared about her well-being. He loved her. She was important to him for reasons not associated with a paycheck. Jackson wanted to know, demanded to know, expected to be kept informed. She wasn't used to that.

"So you've been getting up both morning and evening while I slept to do more work," he stated. He was no longer asking. He was stating fact. "And you have done it quite regularly. You've been missing dinner, and today you missed lunch, again. I don't see you eating breakfast with me very often, and now that I am noticing, you have lost some weight, look drawn and unhealthy. In fact, sweetheart, I haven't had this much awake, daylight time with you in several weeks."

She didn't answer because he was right. She had lost weight, her face was pallid, and she was fielding headaches and dizziness in the afternoons.

"I just needed to get things on a good routine, schedules set, work finished on some projects. I'll be better now."

"Honey, people are worried about you."

"No, that's not it. I'm touchy right now and Josie was feeling a bit burned today."

"Huh, because I didn't get that from her at all when we spoke. She was concerned that you were burning out and was headed for a collapse. She asked me to help you. So, what do you need help with?"

It wasn't turning out as bad as she had thought it would be. He was being rational about this and not spewing edicts. Piper lifted her fork and sunk it into her food again. "Nothing really, I just finished the taxes for the ranch. I got an extension after Pops died but we are doing well now."

"The livestock, GWI, is it all doing well?"

"Yep, all good, but I have to stay on top of it."

"What about your ranch manager? Andy's job is to stay on top of the ranch."

"But not the paperwork." She put up her hand to stop his next words. "But I'm caught up now."

"Great, because I want you to go to Austin. Take your week to work in the GWI office a day or two and take a week off from the ranch. Andy can handle it. I'll oversee things."

She knew she was sporting a look of horror. "I'll lose all the work I've done. I'll be behind again."

"No you won't. The most you'll have to do is pay some bills when you return. I'll stay during the mornings and run it this week."

"No, absolutely not, Jackson. You need to be on your own ranch working it. I can handle this one."

"Listen, we just hired two of the Kirkland boys full time for my place because we expected I would need to take over some here with things as they are. If you buy more cattle at the next auction, there is no way you can do this alone. Not well, anyway."

"I don't want your brothers to get angry about me taking you away. That wasn't the deal."

"I told you we hired two of the boys to take my place and I'm about to offer the other two full-time employment on this ranch. Any objections?"

"No, I think that's great. They're good workers but you need to work your own land. No, I can handle it here."

"Pips, if you don't agree to this help, I'm going to call Rafe and tell him you are in over your head."

"What? That would be a lie."

"Only partly because if you can't keep your head above water without burning the candle at both ends and won't take my help, then you *are* in over your head."

"Fine." She tossed her fork in her plate and was a little disappointed that he didn't react more than a pointedly raised eyebrow. Bratting never got the rise she had hoped with this man.

"Good. Now tomorrow morning you go to Austin, have a spa day, eat in fancy restaurants or order Chinese and watch chick-flicks. I don't care. Sleep late, take naps, and walk in the sun. Do anything, but come back here. I will see you in one week."

"I love that you want me to do that, but I have so many obligations it would be irresponsible."

"It's that or we start maintenance spankings and I'm thinking daily to start."

"What are those and for the record, whatever they are, I don't like them."

He smiled that evil grin she was now always wary of.

"They're spankings that you get on a regular basis to maintain your sweetness and compliance to the house rules that we will be initiating when you return."

"But what if something happens or goes wrong like the shooting?"

"Then I'll handle it. You are allowed one non-emergent phone call to me or Josie each day. That doesn't mean you can do multiple emails either or it won't go well for you." He got up and sat next to Piper, grabbing her hands and bringing them to his lips.

"Baby, I know you want things to work and they are. You have turned this ranch around already and the first quarter isn't over yet. Profits will show, and you'll have the ranch where you want it. Your investments are thriving, and so the only thing that isn't doing well is you. It's time I took care of you.

"As a Daddy, I sucked. I'm sorry I didn't pay enough attention earlier but now I am. I just realized we haven't made love or had sex in a week. That's too long when you sleep next to me. I'm going to remedy that tonight."

He leaned over and kissed her gently at first and then more demandingly, pressing his lips on hers, and forcing hers open as his tongue pushed against her teeth. She did as he wanted and let him inside, inviting his tongue to tangle with hers.

Her little whimper was as enticing as the Siren's call, drawing him in and holding him captive. His shaft answered that call by filling, stiffening, pressing hard against the teeth of his trousers. She reached her hand over to grasp his swelling member and was gently stalled.

"Do we have a deal?" His breath was hot on her cheek.

"Do I have a choice?"

"Sure you do. I gave it to you, spankings or a week off."

"Do I get sex tonight?"

"Mm hm, but do you get it with a good girl or bad girl spanking?"

"I already got a bad girl spanking."

"A small one."

"It wasn't so small. So, I'm getting a spanking regardless, huh? Well, can I pack in the morning?"

"Yes." He kissed her eyelids.

"Okay, I'll go." She brought his lips back to hers.

Chapter 15

He pulled Piper into his arms and kissed her neck. "Strip down, baby."

She started removing her clothes while watching him out of the corner of her eye as he did the same. Jackson was ready when she raced for the shower in her panties and bra.

"No, you don't. I'm giving you a going-on-vacation, you had better mind me, spanking."

"What? No. Jackson, no. I want a shower. You already spanked me."

"Hush, I'm the boss now until you get back and then we will flip for it. You can shower later."

She moaned. "Fine, but no spanking."

"Trust me, you'll love this one. I promise you'll thank me. That is unless you need something a bit more substantial." His implication obvious.

"No," she answered quickly.

"I promise to add sparkle to your evening."

"Mmm, I love those love-making spankings but my butt is already sore." She nodded her head in defeat. "Do I need to turn on the music?"

He laughed. "Josie is at the house with Walker and you're not going to make too much noise." She did tend to be a screamer unless he told her to be silent. "I think we'll try it this way and make adjustments, as needed. We *are* alone."

He brought her to stand with her back to his front. He leaned down and kissed her neck again, tracing her spine with his lips and seeing her shiver with the tickle. His tongue came out, and began exploring the dimples right above the crest of the elastic on her barely-there panties. She trembled. He placed her over his knees.

"I love your panties, baby cakes. They won't prove to be any deterrent at all. I'm going to start now."

He landed an easy swat to her bottom still draped in lace and nylon, rubbing it in slowly. An identical swat to her other cheek was rubbed the same way. Jackson slapped with a little sting on both buttocks before moving his hand in a circle again. The swats came a little faster and harder and his massaging efforts were more intense as he began to remove her panties.

She whimpered. "Um, Jackson?"

"Hold on, honey, I have to get rid of these before I can go on."

He drew the lacy undies slowly down her shapely legs and kissed a trail behind them going down one thigh to her knee and up the other tantalizing leg. He dropped a kiss on both perfectly shaped globes before smacking them twice enjoying the bounce.

Jackson always followed by rubbing and more kissing, his tongue coming out to taste her skin. Piper made little whimpers, wiggling her bottom. Jackson groaned as Piper began undulating in a rhythmic movement as old as man himself. She would be the death of him.

His slaps became more intense as his tongue explored her deep crevice seeking her small, tight opening. Just as a native performer methodically advances the frenzy of her movements in tandem with the increasing tempo of the drum, so Piper escalated her dance of desire in concert with his spanks and tongue. He parted her thighs and tapped them to encourage her further widening to create a great divide.

Jackson felt his breath quickening, becoming as shallow as Piper's. Her urgency was tangible. Her arousal, enticing. He reached down to dip his fingers in her overflowing wetness. She was well prepared for whatever came next.

He hesitated his advance to ask, "What do you want baby?"

"You, I want you. All of you. Please?" She began to lift her buttocks to meet his next slap, and moaned afterwards only to lift her bottom again and again, in anticipation of his hand.

"How does this feel?" He slid his finger in her vagina and then two to mimic the dance his cock wanted to be leading. He scissored his fingers while his other hand slapped her cheeks again.

"I can't do this. Jackson, please take me. I want all of you in me." Her movements were becoming desperate in their urgency.

"Here?" he wiggled his fingers in her hot opening. "Right here, you want me right in here?"

"God yes, please, now. Stop teasing. Hurry, I need you."

While keeping his fingers busy in her steamy opening, he maneuvered his body around. Jackson produced a condom he'd begun carrying ever since his first sighting of her at the funeral. He stood and helped her reposition on the bed, rear facing him. He teased a few more seconds. She whined when he removed his hand from pleasuring her to assist as he ripped the condom package with his teeth. He held his throbbing member in one hand preparing to sheath it. Rolling on the latex he settled into position. He slapped her bottom sharply and as she reared up in response, he pulled her up fully onto her knees and smoothly slid into her waiting entrance.

"I'm here, sweetheart. Hang on. This is going to be a quick ride."

Jackson punctuated that by gliding his cock in hard jabs, tapping her womb several times before slowly pulling almost out again only to shift to another position that he expected to be more gratifying for her.

It evidently did the trick creating a demand in Piper that made her much more aggressive. He loved that. She met his cock, seeking the same detonation that he did, and within a few moments, Jackson knew he was close. He gritted his teeth and slowed, prolonging the exquisite feeling.

She was close and felt incredible, but he knew when she was on the edge. Her little cute-as-hell noises and whimpers were going to put him over all on their own soon with or without her following him. He needed to ratchet her up just a little bit more and then allow her to roll off the cliff.

Jackson prepared to dive off in ecstasy right after her, so he had to hold back now. He reached down to her clit, searching for the magic button to send her rocket into orbit.

The moment his finger came within striking distance Piper wiggled and moaned her need, rubbing him more intently. He felt her hesitate, but he wasn't having any of that. He circled her nub lightly then gave more pressure until she was writhing and then he tweaked it hard as he slapped her ass. She screeched into her pillow as her body shuddered and trembled in rapture.

Two more thrusts into her clenching depths, and Jackson followed her into euphoria. He felt like a randy teenager, because he was almost ready to go another round before he reluctantly withdrew. His baby needed sleep. Maybe they could play again in the morning.

Piper woke to a note on the bedroom mirror.

Pips, I didn't wake you up because I wanted you to sleep. Yes, I turned off your alarm. No, I'm not sorry. Now, give Josie her instructions for the week. I am out working with Andy if you need me. Leave Josie with any information I might need the particulars for, things like deliveries, or better yet, if Josie knows where to find them, then don't bother. Remember, one non-emergency call per day. And if there is an emergency, something goes wrong, or you need me, you had better call. No options to think about. You find you need something other than dinner, call me.

She sighed her contentment. I love you all over, Jackson, but am I *in* love with you? That was the real question of the day. She wasn't sure. She changed thoughts and wondered if she would even be able to relax. It was such a chore to try, she almost didn't but Jackson was right. She needed to relax or crack.

He had already taken things over and Piper was irritated on principal, but in reality, it was odd how she held up her day with a heavy workload. Now that half was gone from her plate, she was more relaxed and more anxious at the same time. Oh, Jackson could handle a monsoon and save her ranch, of that she had no doubts, but she was at loose ends. Right, best thing to do was pack a few toiletries and things, most of her office clothes were still in the condo, and then head to Austin and her offices there. She spoke to Josie and then threw her essentials bag in the back seat of the car.

It would be good to have some time to relax and work on just the investments business. It had been a long time, and even though she'd kept up with the overall movement of the individual portfolios and projects, it had come at a price. it would be nice to just sit in her office and do the day-to-day work.

She was coming to realize that she loved the ranch with the Clearwater Creek running between Gentry and Knight land. It was an integral part of her but not all of her. She enjoyed the investments business equally.

Piper wondered if sometime, she could leave the ranch day to day to someone else, like her husband if that ever happened, and do the GWI day to day. That would be her version of heaven. Jackson was so right this time though. She was tired. Burnt to the proverbial crisp over the grueling schedule she had forced herself to keep. It was unrealistic and if she were to survive, it would have to be adjusted.

Jackson cared about her welfare, showed her he loved her in so many ways, and she thought she might love him. She knew she was in lust, but it was more. When he walked into the room she tingled, and heat rushed through her body like a flash flood. His smile, his body language, the way he winked warmly at her as though they shared a secret, told her she was his and no one else's, and that was heart stopping. So why didn't she jump in head first?

She diverted from going to the apartment and went to the office. She would spend a few hours there and then hit the condo to take a nap and maybe go swimming or set up a spa appointment like Jackson suggested.

Walking into the offices of Gentry World Investments, Piper was swept up in the daily needs of the company. She threw herself in as she did all projects and soon she was saying goodnight to the last of the day staff. All that was left was security and housekeeping. Once again, she was closing up shop alone. Thinking she would call Jackson since she knew Josie would have left already, she felt her sadness balloon when the call went to his voicemail. She checked the clock and knew why. It was nearly nine o'clock, and he was most likely in the shower or already sound asleep. She immediately missed his warmth, both body and soul.

Well, it was a good day of work and she wouldn't come in tomorrow. Best laid plans and all that. She soon found herself in the office by ten the next morning fielding calls from hurt investors. It appeared one of the new hires in the domestic affairs division should have been in supervision longer. Smoothing ruffled feathers and stroking egos took all day. Another day was gone, and she still hadn't gotten one massage or wasted one hour on herself.

Piper answered her desk phone for the hundredth time that day, expecting to put out another fire when a furious voice came over the line only this time it belonged to Jackson Knight. Her chest tightened and her whole body tensed for the verbal spanking about to come her way.

"Piper, think very carefully before you answer this question. Why are you at the office and why at this time of night?"

Silence reigned. She had no problem thinking about the answer, in fact, she would be comfortable to just think about it and not answer at all. Jackson had other ideas evidently because he asked it again.

"I..."

What could she say? He was at her ranch, doing her job there so she could get a break and this is how she thanked him? But didn't he know how hard it was to drop everything? It didn't matter if she made meticulous plans or not, she was a workaholic. She didn't want to be, but she was. Jackson knew that. She was disgruntled that he expected her to do something immediately that was difficult on a good day. He had no right.

"Baby, why? You need rest and some down time. Honey, it isn't healthy."

"I agree but it is a habit I have that isn't something I can just break. There was a crisis, and I was here so I took care of it in the office rather than in the apartment. It took all day."

"Okay, so what did you do yesterday?" When she didn't answer he spoke again. "You spent the day in your office, didn't you?"

"Yes, but the day went so fast it wasn't stressful."

"Okay, when did you go home?"

"About the normal time." She knew how to side step something she didn't want to answer.

"In other words, late. Pips, do I need to come down there and make you relax?"

Yes, she thought, *I want exactly that* but what she said was, "No, I'm not coming in tomorrow at all. I'm having a spa day." Well, as soon as she made the appointment.

"Okay. I'm holding you to that. A spa day is going to make you feel so much better. You know I only want the best for you, honey and you need to de-stress."

"I know. I will tomorrow. Promise." *Well, I promise to try.*

"Okay then. I just have one question."

"Shoot." She mentally thought back to the ranch's needs and prepared for his question.

"Where's the toilet paper? You always kept us supplied but we've run out and well, a man can't do without some things like his woman's warm body and toilet paper."

"Good to know I'm right up there with butt wipe. In the top shelf of the linen closet you should find enough back stock to paper the neighbor's yard."

"Thanks, but I think I'll pass on that because I'd have to clean it up. Okay honey, is everything else going well?"

"Yes. I'm fine."

"Hmm. I hope that's the truth. Okay, then I'll say goodnight. Did you drive in?"

"No, I did a transport car. I'll call for a ride back."

"Good. Love you. Sweet dreams."

"You too," she murmured before she hung up.

Did he notice that she didn't say I love you too? She wouldn't lie about something so important, not to him or herself. But how would she know when she was ready to say the words? Hopefully the revelation came with a full marching band to alert her to the event. She called for her ride and while she waited, she missed her man, exasperating though he was, she wanted nothing more than to curl up against his abs and sleep in the protection of his arms.

Chapter 16

The steam room had been heavenly and now the massage was putting her to sleep so she dozed as the soothing hands of the masseuse enticed her brain to give over to the magic. It had been an exquisite afternoon full of healthy snacks, swimming, relaxation, and pampering. She could sleep for a week. She oozed home, sent a text to Jackson giving him a run down and her plans for sleep. Then she crawled into her bed where she finally slept like a baby, until late the next morning.

Piper didn't really have food in her place, so she munched on dry cereal and coffee until she decided she needed something more substantial. Throwing on some clothing she could wear in public, she grabbed her handbag and set off for the little café around the corner. Then she would stop at the small grocers to get some fruit, yogurt, and a few more things before coming home.

It wasn't a standard meal time, so Piper grabbed a newspaper and sat in a corner table to have brunch, enjoy the financials, the quiet, and revel in the lack of workload. Right after she'd called the office and found life there was uneventful, she settled into her news.

Soon her food was delivered, and she took a bite of the fluffy scrambled eggs, that she then nearly choked on, when Martin Lathrop took the seat opposite her. Two other men as large as the Knight brothers sat at the table next to them. The show of force was impressive, but she would not show any fear. This was a public place, and she had immediately slipped her finger on the record button on her phone. Something she has quickly learned in college cafés.

Swallowing as calmly as she could, she wiped her lips and took a sip of coffee before leaning back in her seat. "If you don't mind, I am having a quiet breakfast alone. If you have anything you need to communicate, then I suggest you speak to my attorney."

"Miss Gentry, I had hoped you would be willing to reconsider your position on selling your property. It is indeed the last section of land that we need to move forward on our build and I am sure our offer was a generous one."

"Generous yes, but why is that? You must understand that even if I wanted to sell, which I assure you I still do not, I would retain the mineral and water rights to the property. Surely you didn't think I would release those or that I was ignorant of the fact that we own those rights." She waited and was gratified when his countenance hardened. "Oh, and I have already filed paperwork to separate the deed of land from the mineral rights and have trussed both up rather tightly. So, as you can see, we have no further business."

"I sincerely hope that is not true, Miss Gentry, for devastating things can happen to a person or their property quite without warning. Some people never recover from the event. I'm sure you are quite aware of the fact, especially given your family's recent loss."

Piper kept her cool when all she wanted to do was toss the hot coffee in his face and gouge his eyes out before turning him into the police. But she knew how to play it cool, even if Jackson thought she needed to work on her poker face.

"Well, yes, I'll keep that in mind. In fact, so others can help me remember your warning, I have a ranching blog now that has shared a lot of the trials of running a ranch and a highly successful investment corporation while dealing with that loss. My family, friends, and readers are growing by leaps and bounds, so to speak. You might even like it. Today, it's going to feature your visit and warning. I hope you don't mind if I use your name. It will be, after all, an accurate account of our meeting and your generous advice. Others might be interested in it as well. It will go well with the other conversations we have had."

"You won't have any proof that any of it ever happened like you say."

"Maybe, but the conversation we are having now has been streamed to my cloud so I've taken care of that problem. I recommend you do as my attorney suggested and not contact me again. If you're on my property again, I will consider it trespassing and a personal threat to my safety. In Texas, they shoot first and ask questions later. Good day, Mr. Lathrop."

The men rose without another word and left knocking over several chairs as they went. Piper brought her tremoring hands up to the table when they'd gone. She had not often felt that threatened or that scared by the actions of another person but there was no denying the sense of fear that she had experienced. The waitress, who had either been paid to go on break or had simply decided she didn't want to interfere, was only now asking if she was in need of anything. Piper asked for her check with all but that one bite of egg left on her plate. If the server thought it was odd, she never said a word but took Piper's card and paid the bill.

Her heart calmed down enough to allow her to dial Rashid in a halfway controlled manner to tell him what had happened. "What if the GWI bought the mineral rights for possible future investment potential?" she asked.

"Is that what you want?" Rashid's tone said it wasn't his recommendation.

"Not really, but what else can I do to keep everyone safe?"

"Let me look at legal ways but don't shoot them for God's sake. I do not want to go to court with you over bloodshed. It isn't even my specialty."

His attempt at humor amused Piper. "Fine but you're taking all my fun away."

"Sorry but necessary. I'll make it up to you with a good outcome."

"Have you by any chance met Jackson?"

"Who? The guy I added to the power of attorney? No, why?"

"Yes, that's him. Never mind, call me when you have something."

Piper didn't feel safe walking back to the apartment, so she called a cab and once she was in it, decided to go to the office. It just felt safer to be around people she was familiar with right now. She knew she should get her car and drive but she hated doing that in the city.

She called Jackson to tell him about what had happened but had to leave it on the voice mail. She tried Josie next, and she didn't answer either. Looking at her watch she knew why. Lately, Walker had taken to having lunch at the ranch. Josie would be occupied. It was a nice day, so she was probably outside. Piper left a message and hoped one of them called her back soon.

After sitting in the office gathering her wits about her, she sent a text to her typical driving service and ordered a pick up. She'd go home and binge on one of the series she liked. When the notification call that her ride was downstairs came in, she grabbed her bag and laptop. She waved goodbye to Leanne and tried Jackson again with no new result. While riding back to the condo, she called Josie who answered.

"Finally a real person, I was beginning to wonder where everyone was."

"I'm sorry Piper. I was having lunch on the patio and left my phone on the kitchen counter. I didn't notice there was a message until I answered your call just now. What can I do for you?"

After recapping the morning and getting Josie to promise to have Jackson call her when she next ran into him, Piper was saying goodbye when she saw smoke ahead. "Oh, wow, there's some kind of fire ahead."

"A fire where, Piper?"

"I'm not sure, close to my condo building. Josie, it *is* my condo building! God, it's in flames and it looks like part of it is gone."

"What do you mean, gone? Like exploded? Are you safe?"

"Yes, I'm safe for now. That's it, exploded. I'm going back to the office. We can't get any closer and everything is closed off. I won't get in there. Go find Jackson. Tell him as soon as I rent a car, I'm coming home. Tell him to listen to my messages."

After contacting the police and giving them her particulars in case they were looking for the residents for head count or something, she had a rental car delivered. She'd decided early in the corporate game to pay mileage on private vehicles instead of investing in company cars and it had proven to be a good move except in cases like this. There wasn't a vehicle to drive back to the ranch.

What could have happened? Why *her* building in the *middle* of the block? And if she hadn't needed the safety of being with others earlier, she would have been in that building on one of the upper floors, trapped, possibly dead. She wondered if anyone had lost their lives in this mess.

The fire happening fast on the heels of the run-in with Lathrop was suspicious. Surely he hadn't done this. Something in the back of her mind told her that he was capable of anything but without one scrap of proof, there wasn't going to be any way she could push that theory. Not yet, anyway.

Piper had just finished giving instructions to Leanne. She'd finished leaving a message with Rashid when Jackson called.

"Jackson?" Her relief was palpable.

"Thank God. What in the hell is going on there?"

"I've got my rental here, can I call you back? It will be about ten minutes. Hold on," she looked at the delivery driver, "Is there Bluetooth?"

He looked like she was crazy. "Yes ma'am, most cars these days are equipped with it."

"Okay, thanks. I'll need you to show me how to connect."

She returned to her phone conversation as she and the driver walked toward the elevator. "Jackson, as soon as I have the car connected to my phone, I'll call you back. But I'm fine. I wasn't there when it happened. I'm good, just shaken up a bit."

"Ten minutes. You don't call me back and I'll have to start in your direction."

"Don't be ridiculous. I'll call you back, but you need to button things up at the ranch. I'll explain soon."

She hung up, not willing to carry the conversation into the elevator or within earshot of another person. Jackson trusted her enough to know she didn't over react, and so would be issuing the appropriate orders, as she prepped and synced her phone. Piper knew she needed to be on the road before she called Jackson back and while he would be testy that he waited he would agree that Austin traffic at any time was distracting but at four in the afternoon on a Friday, it would be near traumatic.

As she pulled through the last busy intersection and hit Highway One, she began to relax her hands on the wheel. She didn't mind the traffic, but she was tense today. Piper thought about what could have happened. Of course if something like the boiler blew, even though she would think it odd in such a well-maintained building, she could reconcile that as simply an unfortunate accident. If someone rigged the place to blow, because there was no doubt with the damage she could see that it was at least one explosion, would she have been the reason people lost so much?

Her phone was ringing, and she knew it was an irritable Jackson before she even looked at the name on the car device. She didn't blame him. She'd said ten minutes, and it had been nearly thirty. She switched lanes and put on her cruise control as she hit the answer button on the steering wheel.

"Hello?"

"Piper, what happened to you?"

"Sorry, nothing, I was longer because traffic was a bit heavy. It's the worst time to be driving through downtown Austin. Have you locked things up as best as you can there?"

"Yes, but I don't mind telling you that I'm confused and worried that you're so uptight still. I thought you had a spa day. What is this about a fire?"

"I did but today erased any good that did me." Piper went on to explain her unexpected and unwelcomed meeting with Martin Lathrop and his goons.

"Why didn't you call me, Piper Kay?"

She rolled her eyes and was glad she was in the car alone. "Don't you start using my middle name to make a point. I have enough of that from Rafe. Now here is the thing. I had to record the conversation, so I was unable to call you at the time. Sorry but I chose the most helpful and useful in the long run. Let's face it Jackson you are a long way from Austin when I need immediate assistance."

"But he threatened you? That little weasel. I'm going to twist his neck so hard his little head will explode."

"Great visual, thanks. I felt threatened, and that's enough. I sent a copy of the recording to Rashid and he's going to get a restraining order executed against the entire company and Lathrop specifically. Anyway, I loaded the blog I wrote afterwards into the cloud but I haven't sent it yet. Rashid wanted me to wait until he had everything through the court. Until then, I need to tell you about the condo."

"Is that where the fire was? Your condo?"

"I bet it's all over the news by now." She knew he walked over to click the news on so she waited. "Am I right?"

"That's your condo going up in flames."

"Yes, that's what I said, it was blown up and the scary thing was, I had intended to return there but didn't. I changed my mind because I didn't want to be alone after the encounter in the café. I literally had the driver change directions after we had gone a few blocks."

"Shit. So, when did the condo thing happen?"

"On my way home from the office, I saw it. We turned around and went back where I called everyone. I expect to be home in about another hour. I'm coming out of Austin suburbia and will be there soon. I don't know what to do but lay low and keep a watch for whatever might happen next."

"What about your office?"

"I told Leanne to send everyone home early and for no weekend work to be done. All deadlines would be extended, if need be, to keep them out of the building. Security is beefing up over the weekend and beyond. I really don't know what else to do right now. Rashid is handling the court and the police. He's fielding the condo thing for me too."

"Honey, how are you, really?" Jackson's voice had changed now that he had all the information. The tenderness was almost her undoing. She was tired, scared, and flaming mad. All she wanted to do was get to Jackson and let him take over for a while.

"I'll make it but I'm anxious to get back and be with you."

"I know. You just get here. I'll take care of everything else. Don't worry Pips."

It was what she needed to hear. When she hung up she did feel more relieved and the further she was from Austin and all the chaos there, the better she felt.

Part way home, she decided to stop for a bathroom run and something to drink. If she were in her car she would have had some water, but... that's when she remembered her cute little car was probably destroyed. The parking garage was underneath the building. She thanked the Lord again for stopping her from going in that building earlier. Once she was there she probably would have stayed creating possibly a very different scenario.

Parking near the front of the large gas station, she ran inside to use the bathroom and grab a bottle of lemonade and one of water before exiting the building. It was a busy place, and she pulled her keys out as she approached the rental car. As she was reaching inside the bag for the water, she dropped her keys. She bent to pick them up. A loud shattering sound echoed in the air, fragments of something hard rained over her and she dropped to the ground.

Next, a thud sounded, like when she had shot game. A screaming, searing pain was racing through her arm. A bullet meeting flesh made a specific sound and the burning heat as it tore through her flesh stunned her.

The next noise was like practice with a tin can only more substantial. Wheels squealed, people were yelling, and all Piper could do was lie on the ground and try to breathe. Someone touched her shoulder.

"Ma'am, ma'am, are you all right?"

Piper looked up into the concerned face of a man around her father's age.

"I don't know. I think so." She tried to get up but the pain in her arm was hot and throbbing.

"No, ma'am, you aren't all right. I think you were shot. It's a sure thing your window is shot out. If a bullet didn't get you, the glass must have. Its safety glass so there shouldn't be any shards."

The man helped her up, and it was obvious that she had been grazed, but not significantly hurt. By the time the police and emergency medical technicians arrived, the blood was down to little more than a trickle, and the burning was subsiding. Piper was shaken up and had put in a call to the car rental and Jackson. She was done for the day. Jackson was about half an hour away if he tore up the roads, forty-five if he followed the speed limit signs. She expected him at any time.

The rental company representative had come to claim their car, and found out they were going to have to wait, so they signed it over to the police for the duration of their investigation and left. Her interview was partway through when Jackson arrived. She was never so happy to see anyone in all her life. To say she was over her coping limit for the day would have been an understatement.

"Piper, you were hurt? Baby, you didn't tell me."

"I didn't want you to get into an accident on your way here. It's nothing, really."

The look he gave her would have given her pause if it wasn't accompanied by his fiercely protective stance. He looked at the policeman and the technician as though they were the enemy.

"When can I take my girl home?"

The question was posed to both men, neither answering right away. Piper had no doubt that if they did not answer as expected, there would be trouble. She was not putting any stumbling blocks between the protector Jackson and anything but his end goal. Her safely with him. She remained silent.

The cop spoke up. "And you are?"

"Jackson Knight, her fiancé."

Both men looked at Piper as Jackson declared his relationship as though to see if she would dispute his announcement. She wasn't about to challenge *this* Jackson on anything. She wanted to go home, and he was the one who was going to accomplish that. With no objections, the policeman continued.

"I'm almost done with Ms. Gentry for now. She says she lives on Gentry Ranch and Gentry World Investments is her corporation." The officer raised his eyebrows at Jackson looking for what? Agreement? The ass.

Piper took immediate exception and could see Jackson did as well. If there were such a stance as pissed off badger supersized, that was her man right now. She thought he would say something, but he didn't. She did not have the strength to do more than internally grumble at the implication.

It was insulting to have the policeman openly verify her words by repeating them to Jackson. The cop was skeptical possibly because she was young, had been shot at, owned a company, was a woman, and more. Any of those things or none of them could have been his reason but Jackson simply gave the cop a blank stare and turned to the medical tech. How could she not love him more for that?

He took hold of her uninjured left hand, turning it over and kissing the palm before speaking.

"Does she need follow up?" He weaved his fingers with hers. She needed that. She wanted to cry, and the comfort was making it hard for her to maintain.

"Not unless she gets infected. I'll tell you what to look for when she's ready to go."

Jackson waited until the officer was done with his questions and then he asked a few of his own. "Was she the only one hurt?"

"It appears so."

"Was it targeted?"

"Like they wanted to shoot at her specifically? We aren't sure but it isn't likely because she's not in her normal surroundings. It was most likely random."

"Even in light of the explosion of her condo today and her threatening conversation with Martin Lathrop?"

"Ms. Gentry didn't mention these incidents to me." Both men turned their attention to Piper. Their faces told her neither was happy with her. "If you don't tell me everything, I won't have the full picture and might not catch these guys."

After filling the officer in on her day prior to this latest incident, she was released to go home. The store had cameras and the phone number Jackson gave was his number. Piper wanted to be irritated but couldn't get up the energy. She just wanted to go home.

Jackson, once she was released, bundled her into his truck, kissed her lips quickly and buckled her seatbelt. Then he kissed her again, this time taking it a little slower before shutting her door.

"Fuck baby. You aren't ever leaving my sight again. I don't think I can handle the strain. I could have lost you today. Not once, not twice but three fucking times."

"It wasn't so much fun for me, either."

"I know. Let's get you home."

Chapter 17

After driving past the new security gate and waiting until it locked behind them before proceeding, Piper was met at the ranch house by those she cared about. She trusted this small group of people and that was a good feeling. It gave her a sense of safety and belonging she needed today. While all the good vibes she was getting from those she had forever added to her list of family was heartwarming, she was not ready to talk to them.

The unspoken questions were loud and Piper swayed as she lifted her foot to take the first step to the front porch. Strong arms wrapped around her shoulders and tucked under her knees to sweep her into them.

"Hold on Pips, let me get you inside."

She wanted nothing more than to do that. She sighed. He held her tighter. Jackson climbed the stairs, and the small group of people parted for him like Moses and the Red Sea. Piper didn't say a word. Her man was taking care of her and while she knew tomorrow she would be fighting every person who tried to steer her away from her chosen path, tonight, she would allow Jackson to be that caretaker. He gently laid her on the couch, kissing her lips again as though to continually prove that she was there with him and safe.

"Okay, as soon as I get Piper settled, we will answer the questions and do what has to be done."

She watched him get a fuzzy throw off the recliner, grab another pillow to support her arm on before wandering into the kitchen only to reappear quickly.

Jackson handed Piper a glass with a small amount of amber liquid in it.

"You're giving me brandy?" Her face lit up. "Have we gone old west?"

"Hell, yeah, baby. Today has put us back in the days of protect your own no matter what."

He watched Piper take a drink and smiled at the disgusted face she made. Good to know his baby hadn't taken up drinking in the over stressed life she had created away from him. He wouldn't have to retrain that out of her, anyway. He set the glass down and marveled again at the beauty that was his woman. She was one tough cookie, but she was allowing him to take the lead because she needed him to take care of her. She trusted he would do it well. He intended to do just that.

He had wanted to build this relationship for years, ever since she finished college and made her home away from him. He knew neither of them was mature enough then to understand the balancing act it would take to achieve this level of success for either of them. The time away was painful but he could see in hindsight, it'd been necessary. But doing it alone was not the answer now. Not for the two of them. It wouldn't happen again if he had anything to say about it. He would show her she could have her company, the ranch and him.

He picked her up, blanket and all, and replaced her on his lap before looking around at those sitting in the room waiting for answers.

"Now, I'm going to fill you in on what has been going on. I'm going to start from the beginning. Chime in if there are any questions because it is going to take all of us to figure this out and come up with a plan we can achieve."

With little fanfare, the whole story was told from the first encounter with Blackwell Corp men through today's events. Questions had been asked along the way, but when the whole story was told and both Jackson and Piper had stopped giving new information, the room sat silent for a full minute before everyone seemed to be talking at once.

Jackson watched the others in the room and something was off. He knew he was likely being hyper-cautious but while Cody had what Jackson believed was the appropriate reactions to the story as it unfolded and correlations were highlighted or implied, Andy seemed different. He wasn't as surprised about the story and even when they talked about what happened today, something was not right.

The part that seemed to affect him was the window being shot out of her rental. Andy was the only one offering differing thinking that this was all coincidence. It seemed that once she was shot at, all other options became irrational against the overwhelming belief that she was being targeted for the ranch. Sawyer had gotten up and walked to the front door, he now turned to whistle loudly into the room.

"All right, so we know things have gotten pretty hot these last weeks and today, someone turned up the heat even further. We have to come up with a safety plan that will allow us to keep on top of the ranches but keep them and everyone safe." He looked at the two women sitting on the sofa with Jackson and Walker. "And you two will need to do what you're told."

"Sawyer—"

"Is right," finished Jackson giving a stern look to his already protesting woman.

Josie spoke up sitting away from Walker as she did. "Sawyer, I understand what you and the others are doing but honestly, we aren't stupid women who can't take care of ourselves."

"I never said or meant to imply that, but what I did mean to say is that you two are not going to do as you please until this issue is safely resolved."

Walker completed the thought. "That means not going against what we have set up to keep you and everyone safe. And there will be no excuses for disobedience." Josie crossed her arms over her chest in a show of defiance, but she didn't contradict him.

"Okay, putting my natural irritation to being in a room with way too much testosterone aside, I have to agree the best thing to do is to work on what next should happen. Plans are best when put together in a calm, rational brain so what are you thinking?"

Jackson rubbed his hand up and down Piper's arm as she spoke. He knew what it was costing her not to take the lead but he also knew she was tired. "Pips right, so what now?"

The plan was put into place. No one went anywhere alone. Jackson, Walker, or Sawyer would escort the women if they needed to go anywhere and the operative word was *need*. Otherwise, while in either ranch house the women could be their own second. Everyone agreed that the house was the safest place for them.

"I guess we could go back to Austin for a while," offered Josie. Her tone wasn't exactly convincing of her desire to do so and the men immediately vetoed the idea.

Cody said, "We'll need to divide and conquer. There's no other way to make this work."

Walker spoke up but looked at Josie. "We can only keep you safe if you are with us and we have two ranches to run now. You women are going to have to do all the inside and office work so we can focus on the outside work."

"Oh, what about Celia, she is supposed to come in twice a week?" Josie asked.

"Call her and cancel for now," answered Piper. "We are not going to be responsible for putting her life in danger for a little dusting and toilet bowl cleaning."

"I agree," answered Sawyer. Even though he was the younger of the Knight men, he'd had a seriousness about him since birth which made it easy to hold his own when Jackson was four years his senior and Walker eight.

Piper nodded. "We need to let the hands on this ranch, at least, know that there is a possibility of some trespassing. If they don't choose to stay, we have to honor that. Should I hire more men?"

Jackson smiled even though there was nothing funny about the situation. If he had ever doubted it she had proven what a leader she was, thinking of those around her first.

"Possibly but let's talk to the men and the sheriff first. I think we can get some guidance, your Rashid will call you back, and then we will decide if we need more men and if there is anything else we can do."

"Well, and I think we can handle it around here without adding more strangers to the mix." Andy seemed agitated, but he was used to a calmer existence with the same routine and workers. Cody agreed with Andy.

"Yeah, I wouldn't want new men unless I had to take them. It makes everything harder at a time when control is important. If you haven't built trust, it's doable, but difficult."

The men were nodding agreement and murmuring their understanding.

Jackson heard Piper mumble something. "What honey?"

"Should I get my guns out?"

"Oh no you don't, young lady. It's dangerous enough without you bringing out additional hazardous items to the mix.

"No, really, I know how to shoot and I don't want to be someone else's responsibility to take care of. It's not like I'm going looking for anyone to shoot down."

"Piper Kay Gentry, if you even try to pull out guns in the middle of this mess I'm going to—" Piper's hand flew to cover his mouth, her eyes wide. She stopped him before he could inform the world that he would blister her ass until sitting would only be a fond memory.

"Okay, I get it," she whispered. He grunted his reply because he intended to review this conversation later tonight.

"Okay, otherwise it is business as usual. I'm hoping we can end this mess quickly, but we have to be smart about it until things are really back to normal." Jackson listened to a few more comments before shooing everyone home.

"Josie is still coming home with me at night. I'll just bring her back every morning."

"Sounds good to me," answered Jackson.

AFTER DINNER, EVERYONE went home in group, leaving Piper and Jackson to settle into their own bed. The days were going to get more intense and the fear that more fallout would be coming their way was an exhausting thought.

Showered and snuggled in Jackson's arms was just where Piper wanted to be. Safe, secure, protected, possessed.

"Jackson? Do you think we are over-reacting?"

He sighed heavily. "Honest? I don't know but my fear is that we aren't. What I do know is we can't risk anything happening to you or Josie and we defend what is ours. I hope the ranch hands that we have are sticking by us. It will be a whole new problem if they aren't."

"I hate we can't prove they did anything. Lathrop helped me to get the restraining order by saying what he did but my heart hurts at the implication that he had something to do with Pops' death."

"Can the restraining order be for you company, your property, and you?"

"I think that is what it will cover but restraining orders aren't very efficient, are they? Rashid thinks it will just paint a pattern of harassment and threats when we ultimately go to court."

"Let's go to sleep baby. I want to make love to you but I'm not sure I have the energy and I'm sure you don't have any. And your arm has to be stinging and achy. Let me help you feel good and relaxed. Take a pain pill and lie still."

"I want to let you but I am finding it hard to let go and allow you free access. I'm tired and want to relax but I can't stop my mind from spiraling out of control."

Jackson slid her night shirt off her belly and up over her breasts, stopping to give those twin beauties some sensual attention before he continued pushing the shirt up.

"Raise your arms baby."

She started to lift up when she heard the slap before she felt the sting. "Ow. That doesn't help me relax."

"I said lay here, not do anything else," he said as he rubbed her inner thigh to soothe his spank.

"How was I to know that you wouldn't appreciate some assistance?"

"Because I didn't ask for any."

Piper didn't say anything to that. She allowed Jackson to tease her nipples, kiss her lips sliding his tongue into her mouth to tangle with her tongue. He kissed her and softly ran his work roughened hands over her skin that was heightening it's sensitivity and she allowed herself to fall into the sensations.

His hands and lips continued downward to connect with her pubic curls. His low gruff tones as he started to tell her how beautiful she was.

"You are so damn sexy, Baby cakes that sometimes I am afraid of the strength of feelings I have for you. The need that gnaws at me every time I see you, smell you. It's embarrassing to me that I can be so vulnerable when I'm with you. But I wouldn't any of this up for anything."

"I thought I was the only one who felt that way."

"Oh, sweetheart, you aren't the only one. I promise you."

His tongue swooped into her arousal slickened pink bits beneath her puffy inner folds.

She arched sliding her hands where his tongue was. "Oh, Jackson."

"Piper Kay, you are so naughty. If you have to have your hands in the midst of the fun, you will get a job. Hold your lips open for me. I want you full accessible."

"What? Jackson," she whispered, "I can't do that."

He slapped her inner thigh just hard enough to get an answer whimper. "Daddy, and you will do it, or I stop and spank you instead of getting you off."

Another whimper but she slid her hands back down and held open her lower lips for him.

"Nice. Hold on baby."

Jackson put one hand on her nipple, massaging and tweaking, the other in her channel, entering her and circling her clit. His hands were gentle, insistent, hitting all her sensitive areas with just the right pressure.

The pressure was building, she was growing hot, antsy, and her peak suddenly slammed into her without further warning, stealing her breath. Jackson continued until he had squeezed out every drop of her orgasm.

Without a word, he kissed her lips, her cheek, her shoulder then drew her into him tight spooning her securely.

"I love you with all that I have, Piper Gentry."

"I love you too, Daddy." She yawned and he laughed.

"Go to sleep baby. Sleep."

Chapter 18

The next morning, Piper listened again to Jackson as he gave her instructions on what she was supposed to do in case of an emergency. He made her check her phone for a charge even though he had supervised her charging it last night. Finally, before he left he pulled her tight to him and kissed her hard.

"Pips, I know you are a force to be reckoned with in the boardroom, but here sweetheart, we are living a different reality. We handle the threat a different way. Now, get on the phone and make your calls. I'll check back in to find out what the outcome is but under no circumstances do you leave this house without male escort. And if you need to leave, it had better be for a damn good reason. You got me?"

Piper made the inadvisable response of rolling her eyes couched in a heavy sigh. "Ouch, dammit, Jackson Knight, that hurt like the devil." She was frantically rubbing her butt and backing away from its attacker.

"Push me and I'll go into full Daddy mode and you will be sorry you forced it on yourself. You got me?"

"Yes. But I'm capable of taking care of myself. I've had to take care of me and others for a very long time."

"Have you been shot at before?"

"No."

"House blown up?"

"No."

"Bullied and threatened by goons?"

"Okay, no, alright?"

"Then you understand why I'm just a little bit protective and why you are going to listen to me and do exactly as I tell you."

"Fine."

He pulled her into his arms. "This is serious, Piper. If you intend on not taking me seriously then we can have a full-blown whipping right now."

"No, no, that's fine. I know it's serious, but I don't like being treated as though I can't take care of myself."

"I get it. So you promise to follow the rules and I promise not to shove them down your throat."

She nodded. "Deal."

Jackson leaned down and kissed her hard again, holding her close while she breathed in his scent. Yeah, she loved this man but did she love him enough? He deserved a woman who would give him as much devotion as he gave her, and Piper wasn't sure she was ready for that. She'd declared herself last night but then she fell asleep.

Better to keep things to herself a while longer until she was sure and the danger was passed them. Until then, she would show him in as many ways as she could that she only had eyes for him.

Piper hit the disconnect button on her desk phone. She looked up and encountered Josie's look of inquiry. "Not a good outcome?"

"No. The judge agreed for the restraining order against me, my company and my ranch since I don't have my Austin place anymore that about covers it. But the Sheriff, other than keeping a copy of the restraining order and accepting a picture of Lathrop, that is all I get."

"You'd think a restraining order would get more involvement."

"Yeah, well the sheriff tells me that there are too many of them to enforce actively. If we have a problem, he said to call him. He'll send someone out."

"So, we are on our own."

"Yep. Keep working on those projections I gave you because the cattle auction is next week. I'll be back in a few."

Piper was glad that there was no questioning of where she was going or what she was doing by Josie. Walker must have been pretty intense with her before dropping her this morning because she'd been careful to ask every other time. At least she wouldn't have to lie to her.

Piper slipped out of the door before she realized that she didn't have her car any longer. Going back inside to grab the keys to Pop's old pickup, she hoped it would start, and remembered it was a manual transmission when she got inside. She'd learned on one but as soon as she had been able, she'd bought a car with automatic transmission. She put it into gear praying she didn't strip the gears and miraculously, it slid easily into reverse and then first gear. She headed to town to buy some needed supplies.

Walking out of the gun shop, which is the only place in town that sold bullets, she had new gun cleaning accessories and lots of ammunition. As she was pulling back out of the parking lot, her cell went off, so she re-entered the slot she was exiting and answered the phone.

"Piper, where are you?"

"I'm in the truck on the way home."

"Oh, geez, I'm sorry but when I found Andy in the office again when I came back from the bathroom and couldn't find you I told him to get out. He got all kinds of ticked off and said it was his office long before it was mine or yours. I still couldn't find you, so I called Walker. I'm so sorry, he got hold of Jackson and I'm pretty sure he'll be here soon."

"Maybe he'll just call."

"Yeah, maybe." Josie sounded anything but convinced and Piper agreed it was not likely. She hung up and started back to the ranch.

Things would be a bit dicey if Jackson got there before her.

Piper put the truck in its spot and looked for Jack's truck. Luckily it wasn't there. She raced inside and started for the bedroom. "How was your trip?"

Damn. Stopping mid step, Piper turned toward the owner of the cold voice. "What?"

"Is that bag from the gun shop?"

She looked as though she didn't know what was in her hand. She raised the bag slightly. "Yes."

"Did you go there today? Alone?"

"Yes."

"I see. Well, you'd better put it in the bedroom."

Piper was suspicious of the man who stood before her acting as though nothing was wrong, except his face told her everything was wrong. She headed for the bedroom and when she would close the door, it wouldn't close. It hit something. Piper didn't have to look.

It was Jackson's foot. She turned to face him again.

"Jack—"

"Keep going."

"No, really, I spoke to the sheriff, and he can't help."

"Piper Kay Gentry, get your ass inside."

"Fine but you aren't going to... um, I'm not okay with..."

Big hands turned her around and then landed on her nearly unprotected rear end, hard and fast. Just as much as she was used to Jackson responding quickly and without much fanfare when he was intent on communicating his displeasure, she was equally surprised every time his large hand connected with her ass. Multiple times.

After what felt was no less than fifty intensely direct smacks that seemed to go over and over the same sorry spots, all administered while he had her leaned over his powerful arm, she quit fighting him.

How he was able to hold onto her thrashing body while he landed his punishment with incredible accuracy, she had no idea, nor did she care until the thought dawned on her that he did it because he loved her.

The tears began to come to the surface. Each time he laid a sizzling swat to her throbbing rear, her only thought had been outrage at the audacity of the man to take her to task. But when she realized she must have frightened him, again, she knew he was frustrated. He resorted to the only other way he knew to communicate his fear to her in a way that she would listen. This was the only thing that got him results.

She stopped flailing, and he stopped spanking. In her fury, she hadn't felt the true effect the man had wrought on her bottom. Now that she had stopped struggling, the full manifestation of his rampage on her butt was immense burning and throbbing. And with the realization that the man loved her so much he was willing to risk all to pound what he hoped was sense into her, brought that familiar tingle to her nose and fat hot tears filled her eyes.

She knew without a doubt that if she laid down for him, her channel would be slick enough to accept him without any further efforts on his part. Whether she had wanted to admit it or not, Jackson and all of his Neanderthal ways excited her. Not that she would ever admit to it in a court of law, but maybe under cover of darkness.

"Now what were you saying you were not okay with?" asked Jackson as though they had not had an interruption in their conversation.

"That. I'm not okay with it." The conviction and volume were all but gone from her voice.

"Too bad, because I'm not okay with you throwing all precaution out the window the minute the thought occurs to you. We had an agreement, didn't we?"

"Yes. I know," her voice remained quiet.

"Good. Now tell me why you decided to go against what I expressly told you to do. What we *agreed* on."

She ignored his question to answer another unvoiced one. "I know I scared you yesterday when I was shot at." She shrugged. "And everything else that went on. Then today, when I went into town alone you were scared again only this time it was my fault."

She moved the heavy bag with her foot from the center of the floor where she had dropped it during the spanking and sat on the bed, deflated and dejected. Her hiss declaring the effectiveness of his discipline.

"I'm sorry. I didn't think things through. I didn't think about what I was doing to you."

She dared to glance into his eyes that bored into hers and she felt connected. The tears, which had been on the surface since her ordeal began yesterday, came rushing forward overflowing their appointed boundaries. As if on cue Jackson gathered her into his strong arms. The very same arms that had used their strength to hold and spank her to communicate his fear clung to her tightly, shielding her from the cruelty of the world. Piper hadn't realized how much she craved that feeling of security at the hands of another. No, not another, Jackson. She wanted him to always be there for her.

"I know baby. I know you don't like discipline, but you have to understand why I do it. I can't even contemplate life without you in it, and now that I have you in my life again, I'm never letting go. So when you disregarded me, I had to impress upon you the real need to pay attention, to be careful. And this is a method I know works."

"Jackson, I'm just so frustrated at the lack of legal avenues to protect oneself from further harassment and harm than we have already gotten. There is no way we can expect the sheriff to get out here soon enough to help if we need it. The restraining order was granted but it relies on law enforcement to act. We don't have the confidence of that. I'm not used to not being able to control the outcome of a situation."

He let her sit down again and rubbed the back of his neck as he paced the room. "It's not his fault really. We are too far for that kind of help. But it was stupid and irresponsible to go out unprotected this afternoon."

"No, the sheriff was in the next building."

Jackson ran his fingers through his hair in frustration. "Yes, but then you needed to travel without protection, or did you forget yesterday afternoon so soon?"

Piper's voice was not so strident now as it had been before being disciplined. "No, I know it was a risk, but I couldn't wait."

"I hope it was worth it darlin' because tonight, Daddy's going to set your fanny on fire again."

"But you already spa... did." Her outrage at a repeat performance was couched in a whine she didn't want to admit hearing, even to herself.

"That was my stress reliever and to help me come down from the events of the morning fear fest. The punishment comes later."

"But I'm an adult."

"Who should have known better than to do what she did. I'm well aware of the fact that you aren't happy with me, but I'd rather that then you coming up hurt or worse."

"Can we talk about this later? I need to find out why Andy was in my office again."

"I wanted to talk to you about that, too. That's why I know about you leaving at all. I got a call from Josie and she was not feeling good about his answer to her."

After Jackson had aired his concerns they agreed to not mention anything more about today but to watch him closer.

Neither wanted to think that he had anything to do with what was happening, but they would be fools not to consider the possibility.

"Let's see if Josie has any ideas on lunch before I go back to work. I'm starving."

"Sorry I worked up your appetite."

"And we are going to do it again later."

Jackson grabbed Piper by the hand and pulled her behind him to find food. Feeling subdued due to the events of the morning, she gave no resistance.

Andy stormed out of the ranch house heading for his place. It was a small bungalow but since he didn't have anyone living there with him, it was plenty for his needs. He'd hate having to leave this place, for the comfort factor alone, but unless some miracle happened, it would be obvious he knew about too many things.

They might not figure out that he opened the door for the invasion of the Blackwell company, or that he had been the pathway to the sudden death of Garth Gentry, which he regretted sorely, but they would figure out enough to make him unwelcome.

He'd been treated well in the Gentry home. In some ways, he'd always thought that it would be his home someday. All he had to do was wait out Garth. He'd fallen in love with Janine Gentry soon after hiring on but she had made it clear that he didn't stand a chance with her.

Later, after she died, nothing but getting the ranch seemed to matter to him. Piper coming back from college on weekends and then Jackson Knight nosing in, getting chummy with Garth had threatened to ruin everything he had worked for.

Andy first had encouraged Jackson to give Piper some space and had convinced Rafe that his sister wouldn't have a chance at a future if she didn't go outside of the ranch and Jackson. Rafe had wanted to be the big brother so he pushed for her to gain some independence. It had worked. She found she had a whole world waiting for her. The ranch became less important and Jackson had been left behind.

Then Andy had done everything he could to get Garth to see that with each of his kids busy with their chosen lives, it would be best to leave him the ranch. The kids didn't even care and he would give them a piece of the profits if he had to. Finally, he had tried to show that the ranch was no longer profitable, encouraging Garth to leave more of the decisions to Andy.

Things were going so well. Garth would have come around eventually. That all went away when Andy made a deal with the devil in the form of Blackwell Investments.

What he didn't know was that they would kill Garth for the mineral rights which the rancher cared nothing about, but that he retained so no one would destroy his land.

After Garth's death, when it was obvious that Piper was determined to keep the ranch and even making it more profitable, he didn't know what to do. Those Knight boys were getting in the way more than he would have liked, and they weren't just country bumpkins. These boys had an education and some deep common sense that was making it hard to get around them. And he'd never seen such a group of protective men in his life. It made them ferocious.

Now Blackwell was becoming more dangerous and more demanding. Andy didn't know about computers, access information, and a whole lot of other things they were asking for.

Now Jackson had changed the access code for the front gate and he didn't even know how to get in and out without help. He knew cattle, and this was getting too far out of hand.

Problem was, he was in too deep. No, Piper would have to go. Then Jackson would leave things alone, Rafe and Rosie would sell and while he wouldn't get to keep this ranch, the money he would come away with was enough to buy his own place and he would finally get what he wanted.

~~

Jackson talked to his brothers after lunch. "Something's not right here. It just doesn't make sense that Blackwell would know to find her while she was on her way home yesterday. I mean, wouldn't they expect her to stay in town? And the rental car was an unknown."

Sawyer shook his head. "I don't know man, but we need to figure things out quickly."

"Okay, let's look at this thing like Piper, more clinically." Walker reached in his back pocket for his little notepad. He had taken a lot of guff over the years for having one at the ready, but it often came in handy. He grabbed his pen out of his vest pocket.

"Now, who knew what happened yesterday with Piper and when?"

After the men had systematically gone through the events, timing, and people involved, it was obvious that the one name they saw was bothersome. Josie had known everything there was to know, when it happened, and it looked like she was the leak except for one vital thing, she did not know about Piper renting a car and coming home when she did. Only Jackson knew that information. Jackson knew first, followed by Andy after Jackson asked him to button up the ranch.

The foreman had asked and Jackson filled him in. He never filled Josie in on his last conversation with Piper before she left Austin. Any information about her whereabouts was given as he was leaving to pick Piper up.

"Okay, so we found the common thread, now what? I mean, we can't just go tackle the man and turn him over to the sheriff with a smile. There isn't any actual evidence." Sawyer was right.

"Let's just fire him." Walker looked at the others.

Sawyer shook his head. "Much as I would like to say that would end our problems, it won't because then he'll have nothing to lose by doing his worst. No, we need to bait him somehow."

"Draw him out? If we don't know what he wants, we don't know what to use as bait." Jackson ran his hand behind his neck to rub the irritation out. No one answered him, and he looked up to see his brothers looking past him. Jackson turned.

"Use me."

Chapter 19

"Dammit, Piper Kay, what are you doing here and where is your escort?"

"Again, with the middle name? Josie's inside the house looking for Walker, but I decided to come outside, and I heard you boys talking. Use me as bait. Blackwell wants me and so Andy needs to find a way to produce me. I'll have Andy come with me either on the ranch or to town or something. That will draw out anyone you need."

Jackson looked at his woman as though she had grown two heads and a pointy tail. Her voice was calm and focused. She wasn't saying anything in the heat of the moment. She was serious.

"No. We will find another way. Go back to the house, baby."

"You can't dismiss me like I'm a child, Jackson. I'm staying and I say I'm the best straight line to solving this mess."

"Piper, I don't think he is dismissing you, but throwing away the idea that you be used as bait. It isn't going to happen on our watch. We are trying to keep you safe. What makes you think we would expose you purposely to danger?"

Sawyer had looked at her as he spoke. Jackson knew his brothers saw her as the sister they never had, and were as protective of her as they would have been if she were born to their mother. It was good because he planned on making that a reality, but it was bad now, because they were going to shield her even if she didn't want the protection.

"I'm willing to concede that it isn't the best idea so if you boys come up with a better plan, I'm all for it. I'm no martyr for the cause but I do want there to be an end to this madness. So, what are your ideas?"

"I don't have any right off hand, but I'll think about it while I work a little longer. I've got a few things I need to do." Walker nodded to his brothers and walked away.

"And what about you?" asked Piper as she stared at Sawyer.

"I'm in the same boat as Walker right now, but we will figure things out tonight. I've got things to finish before I call it a day, too. See you in a few hours. And Piper?"

She looked into Sawyer's face. "If you do anything without our full consent and protection and you survive it, Jackson will not be the only Knight brother that paddles your ass raw."

Piper watched Sawyer leave and looked over at the last brother and waited. "He is speaking the truth. As far as they are concerned, you are as good as their sister and there will be a line waiting to whale on your behind if you go against us." Jackson nodded. "Okay, so we haven't come up with a plan yet but you, young lady, are not going to be part of the implementation no matter what that plan is. Did you lock up the house?"

"I hate I have to do that but yes, I locked it. I'm serious Jackson, I can help. I'm the most logical choice."

He pulled her into his arms and kissed the top of her head. He rubbed her back. God he loved this woman even as she exasperated him. He figured if she didn't affect him strongly, his love was nothing to boast about, but since he had begun to lose mountains of sleep over her, he figured it was the real deal.

"Not happening. Now, go inside with Josie. I'll go back over to your place because I have some breeding schedules to work on. If I do them there, I'll be able to keep an eye on things while sitting in the office. We'll eat here tonight. Did you get what you needed done?"

"I guess but I can't think daily work right now."

"I know, so why don't you help Josie figure out dinner, yeah?"

"Yeah."

"We will work this thing out baby, I promise. But until we do, stay away from Andy and stay indoors as much as possible."

"I will."

"And lock the door."

"Okay."

"And don't—"

She leaned back away from him and put her hands on his chest before looking into his face. "Jackson Knight, don't you have things you need to do?"

"Say yes, Daddy."

"Yes, Daddy."

His smile was quick when he dropped a kiss on her lips and stepped away. "Good girl. Point taken. See you soon, baby cakes." He walked away determined to figure this out so she wouldn't be in danger any longer than absolutely necessary. What scared him the most was that her suggestion might be the best way. He wasn't going to contemplate that right now.

Piper couldn't get the idea out of her head, that if she got Lathrop to think he could get what he wanted out of the way, then they would catch him because he would lower his guard thinking he caught her unawares. She began to come up with a plan to lure Lathrop and his goons out. If Andy was the way to do that, then it would be difficult to pretend she didn't feel complete and total betrayal, but she would do it. She needed her life back and her security reinstated. The safety of the whole ranch and those she loved depended on her getting this right.

That evening, after much debate that only included the Knight men, Rafe telephonically, Piper, and Josie, the only thing decided was that Piper was not to be the bait. Every male agreed upon it and both female participants knew she wasn't that fragile, but they simply gave up the fight.

Later, that night, Piper and Jackson seemed too tired and preoccupied to enjoy each other's more physical attributes, but as Piper tried to settle down, her body just wouldn't relax. Jackson reached over and pulled her close to him.

"No spanking tonight, honey. Just relax. We are too stressed to deal with maintenance but that day will come. It just isn't here yet."

When she still couldn't settle he rolled her front to his front, and began to slowly caress the agitation out of her. He kissed her temple and breathed deeply.

Piper lived for times when he gently loved her like this.

The tension in her muscles released and her mind quieted as he continued to knead her back and neck, rubbing and touching her bottom and the tops of her thighs. She knew with one detour, Jackson would have her right on the edge of sexually responding but with his carefully chosen path, she was only mellowing, relaxing. She smiled and snuggled in tighter, throwing her left thigh over his and promptly fell asleep.

The next morning, Piper awoke to Jackson dressing in the near dark. "It's kind of early, isn't it?" she asked with her sleep laden croaky voice.

"I tried not to wake you. Yeah, it's early baby. Go back to sleep. I said I'd ride fence this morning and go early before the sun kills us. I'll be home around midday." He slipped his boots on now that she was awake. "Do not go anywhere. I have a leather strap just waiting to be useful again. Don't be the reason I pull it off the wall."

"I won't." She presented her cheek for his kiss, but he took her lips. "Aww, I have morning breath, Jackson."

"Hmm, I didn't notice. Now go back to sleep." Then he was gone.

Sleep was not going to come now that her mind was awake. She laid there for a while before deciding that even the soft warmth was not going to entice her to sleep again. Throwing back the sheet and light bedspread, she brought her legs around to the floor and got up. The bathroom was calling her and once in there she decided to take a shower.

Jackson took one every night and almost never took one when he woke up unless they had been extremely amorous in the morning. That didn't happen as often as he would have wanted but what person would get up at the butt crack of dawn if they didn't have to? She loved a morning shower and an evening bath. One woke her up. The other put her to sleep. She even had different soap for both.

When she was dressed and ready for the day, she made a quick effort to make the bed for Jackson. He liked it made; she didn't care. They were so different in a lot of ways except the important ones. He flipped her switch just walking into a room and he automatically searched to find her when he entered a space he knew she should be in.

That man could bring her to orgasm with a look. She knew he stood half erect most of the day. If she wanted something, he weighed the outcome against her satisfaction. She pushed him and he pushed back but they were learning the art of compromise in their relationship. That is what they had, a relationship, and she wanted it to last. She could make concessions like fixing the bed. Maybe he would make one like keeping the strap on the tack wall when he found out what she was going to do today. And he would find out.

Josie came out of the kitchen with a cup of coffee and a plate of eggs, bacon, and toast. "You don't have to cook me breakfast, but I appreciate it."

"I know, but I like to make it for the guys in the morning and so I make enough to bring it over for you. Jackson has usually eaten at the house but if I don't see him there, I bring it over here for you both."

"I bet he was up too early for even you today."

"Yeah, he ate the rest of last night's cake and had two cups of coffee. It should last him until lunch. The sugar alone should keep his motor running that long." The women laughed.

"Josie, I have to ask you something."

The look she got in return was cautious. "Piper, I don't like the sound of this already, and I don't know what the "something" is."

"Since we aren't going to get much help from the law enforcement side if we just wait around, I propose helping things out some."

"The guys said absolutely not. Piper I don't mind telling you that Walker and I are getting serious. I can't afford to mess that up until I know if we are the real thing or not."

"You won't. You'll be the good guy. That is if you don't tell them the rest."

"The rest of what?"

"The rest that says I'm going to catch me a criminal."

"How and please don't say by using yourself as bait."

"You let me figure that out. Now your part is easy. When you see me and Andy drive away, you can call Jackson and tell him that you are worried because Andy and I have just gone into town."

"Piper, Walker told me to stay away from Andy."

"I know but he's the key. He's got to be."

"But what if he isn't?"

"What, the connection? Then nothing will happen, and I'll get something at the store and come home."

"And get us both in trouble."

"Nope, I'll have to endure Jackson's irritation, but you will be the good girl."

"I don't like this."

"I know. Me either, but it has to be done. Now, let me go out to talk to Andy."

"No, I have to go with you if you leave the house. My butt is definitely on the line for that."

"Fine, I'll call him."

Andy grumbled but he agreed to go after lunch. Piper knew that Jackson or any of the guys could be over to eat as was their habit since Josie started making lunch. She didn't want her to give the plan away, so she told a little white lie.

"Okay, we're set for after lunch, tomorrow. He wouldn't go today."

The relief was clearly written on Josie's face. Yeah, that girl was too transparent. Not a good poker player or negotiator. Piper had no doubt that if she did wait until the next day, all three men would be in on her little plan before the next morning.

Lunch was free and easy. Jackson walked in as the group was just diving in and he washed up before sitting next to Piper.

"I see you have managed to stay out of trouble for an entire morning, baby. I'm proud of you."

"I still think you should take me up on my offer."

"Not happening. What are you doing the rest of the day?" he asked as he piled his plate high with chicken and dumplings. It was one of Jackson's favorite meals. Piper didn't answer his question. If he noticed, he didn't say anything.

Things went as well as expected and lunch was soon over with the men out to do whatever was next on the long list of chores they always had at the ready. While others had a routine of chores, the Knights did whatever was needed. Running up to her room, she called Andy who had gone from grumpy to almost cheerful. Piper hoped she knew why and hoped she was wrong all in the same breath.

Andy was the one who had shown her how to do so many things on the ranch. As a young girl when her dad was busy, she followed Andy and whatever cowhand he had with him. She knew he was slowed down by her and as she grew older, she didn't want to cause him undue irritation so she watched him from the tree line or picked plums and berries near him. She watched him inoculate and breed cattle, and along with her dad, they had butchered hogs, gentled ponies, harvested hay, and repaired tack together.

The thought of tack drew her out of her nostalgic wanderings because the use of tack on her ass was in her future but at least, with any luck, it would be a future free of fear that someone was targeting her for her land, mineral rights, or whatever it was they wanted.

When Andy pulled up outside, she yelled to Josie that they were leaving. She hated that she had not been able to get a new car yet, but that would change after today.

"What? I thought you said tomorrow."

"Sorry, I didn't want you to give me up before I had a chance to make this work. You are too honest."

"I don't want you to go. Piper I've changed my mind."

"No problem, call the guys whenever you feel the need. See you soon!"

She had smiled as she left the house but inside she was screaming that it was stupid, and she didn't know what she was doing. She reached inside her bag to make sure she had her small handgun, and felt the reassurance of the fully loaded cold metal of her Glock. She had shopped for a while, comparing holds and comfort before deciding on this one. She never regretted the choice. Today, if she had to, she was prepared to use it for more than practice.

"What's up with Jackson lately? You two have a tiff?" Andy tried to smile as though making conversation, but Piper was not new to the game. She played along.

"He's grumpy these days because of all the hype over me getting shot at, threatened, and my home and car blown up, and then burned to a crisp. He'll get over it when he figures out I'm right. They're just coincidences."

"Sounds like you've changed your tune from a few months ago. There does seem like quite a few of them, though." He kept his voice well-modulated and if she weren't looking for it she would have missed his fishing for her real reactions and information.

There was nothing casual about his remarks.

When she didn't answer, instead of leaving his statement as rhetorical, he repeated it. "So, you aren't worried that anything is really going on?"

"I would be awfully paranoid to think someone was after me. I mean, just because Pops told Lathrop he wasn't selling and then got worried, so he took core samples. Which my attorney says is now properly recorded, and the ownership is granted to all us kids, our kids, and so on. If something happens and we are all killed in some apocalypse or something, then it goes to the Knight boys. Besides, no one can sell it anyway or use the mineral rights."

"What? No one can sell or use the mineral rights?"

"Well, I can, but there is this involved process. So, anyway, I'm not worried. It's all the normal stuff, I guess."

"You can't sell or trade or anything?"

"No one can."

"I'll be dammed." Just as Andy went silent ahead of them was a truck pulled over on the side of the road with its hood up.

"I wonder what's going on here?" Andy didn't even look in the direction of the truck but pulled off to the front of it. "I'll get out and see."

Before she knew it, he was out the door and had shut it. She clicked the lock on the side panel and grabbed the keys he had left in the still running truck. If he noticed she'd turned it off, he didn't come back to check. She dialed 911 and prayed she was close enough to town to get a fast response.

"Nine-one-one, what's your emergency?" She said she was being held against her will and described the truck. "Don't talk. Put your phone on mute and just listen. They're coming."

She shoved the phone under the seat and sat with her hand on her gun inside her purse. She felt for the safety and knew she'd taken it off because her instructor had been a big one for keeping the safety on until you are ready to shoot then knowing when you take it off.

Lathrop and another man approached the car but no Andy. Her heart was pumping so fast she was sure it would explode. Her lungs constricted as she tried to calm her breathing. The acid in her stomach she didn't know was there began a burning path back up her esophagus. Her chest hurt. *Breathe. You have to inhale and exhale.* The man with Lathrop knocked on the window next to her. She screamed. The tremors wracked her body.

Get control of yourself. Even if you had to you wouldn't be able to shoot with your hand shaking so much. Get a grip. But the pep talk did nothing when the man rapped on the window again.

"Open the door."

"Why? Who are you? Where's Andy?"

"He sent us up here. He's having a look to see what's wrong with our vehicle."

"He's no mechanic."

The gun came out to do the talking next. "Open the door."

She reached in her handbag ready to pull out the Glock when she could hear the sheriff's emergency sirens. She laid on the car horn, rolling to the floorboard of the front. It hurt when she landed on the center floor, but nothing would entice her to get up. Someone was trying to break the side window but finding it a challenge. Thank goodness for safety glass.

She could hear a number of vehicle doors open but none shut. The banging had stopped only to be replaced by yelling. Was that Jackson's voice? She couldn't stop shaking and then she heard gunfire right over the hood of the truck. Or at least she thought it was that close. It stopped. There was only one additional shot, more yelling, the truck was being hit by something or someone and finally it was quiet. The silence frightened her more.

The driver's window had someone knocking on it now. Piper was afraid to look. It could have been the man from the other side.

"Piper, baby cakes, it's me. It's Jackson. Open the door honey. It's okay. You're safe."

"Jackson?"

"Yeah, baby, it's me. Open the door."

She reached for the button and pushed it. The door lock released and before she knew it, fresh hot air rushed in, and large hands were reaching under her arms. She was being pulled out of the awkward position on the floor. Her next thought was how familiar and comforting Jackson's scent was. Then she burst into tears.

Chapter 20

It seemed like another lifetime since she had left the scene on the highway, but in fact it had been only a week. An incredibly long, exhausting week, but today it was finally done. Well, Rashid said there would be more to do when the case went to court, but other than testifying, her interviews were over.

It was a trying week where after finding out their foreman's throat was cut right behind her, she paid for Andy's body to be cremated and left the ashes for his nephew to do with as he saw fit. For now, the outside world was satisfied but Piper's personal relationships were in the toilet. Flushed.

Josie had been unnaturally quiet all week, and she asked if she could go back to Austin. "I don't think I'm cut out for being your assistant, Piper. Sorry."

She had left this morning. Walker had yet to say one word to Piper since he was sure she was safe. Piper had no doubt he blamed her for Josie leaving. It was blame well placed. Rafe would be here later today, because after hearing the events involving his sister, he arranged to return home. She left him a note on the desk.

Leanne promised to come to the ranch this weekend with a truck and pick up all her equipment to return to Austin. She checked into a long-term hotel while she looked for a new condo. She had thought that wouldn't be necessary, but it was. It had been a long few months, but it was over, and she needed to get back to normal. She released a humorless sound. Life would never be normal again. What it was now would be her new normal, but no one would consider it within the realm of expected everyday life.

Jackson was still technically staying with her in the house, but he left right at dawn and returned to grab a bite, shower, and sleep in the guest room. She left him a note on the bed he now slept in. He could go home again to resume whatever life he wanted, without her. After all the fighting she had done to keep the ranch and make it a go, it was making excellent profits but now she wouldn't come back. She told Rafe in her letter he could sell. She would never come back.

She climbed in her new car and while she missed her old one, this SUV was more sedate. The wild, adventurous woman who had been excited to buy her first new sports car was gone. In her place was a disillusioned woman, who had lost the best things in her life. She'd thrown them away like they had no value. The sadly ironic thing was, this time last year, she would have said these nonmaterial parts of her life, her relationships, were the most important but she didn't live her life that way. She thought she'd learned better, but obviously she wasn't a person who valued others.

She even questioned whether she was qualified to run GWI any longer. Obviously, her perceptions were off, and it would only follow that if she were out of touch with the world around her and how it functioned cohesively, she would not be connected enough to make good investment choices.

Newsflash! This is what depression feels like Piper. Yeah, well get used to it for you will never be completely happy again. Was it possible that she would even welcome Jackson's spankings if she could be assured of his love and devotion for the rest of her life? Without a doubt, she would love him regardless of what he demanded and do whatever he expected, but in her heart, she feared it wouldn't matter.

She checked into the hotel and went to her room. She had just paid the doorman and shown him out when her cell rang. She saw it was Rafe. He must be at the ranch by now. She considered not answering but that wasn't her style so she clicked yes and pushed speakerphone.

"Hello Rafe, did you get in safely?"

"Yes, I'm in the office. I guess you intended to be gone when I arrived." His voice was a little chastising. Her lips wiggled in some amusement. He would always be her big brother.

"Sorry, I thought it would be for the best. You were right. I made a royal mess of everything." She might as well get it out of the way.

"I never said that and to look at the numbers you sent us a couple weeks ago, you have performed a small miracle pulling the ranch out of a slow nosedive. Really, it was impressive given the obstacles you had to overcome. I'm sorry you had to deal with Andy and all, alone."

"I didn't do it alone. I had Jackson, well the Knight brothers and Josie to help me. But it was more adventure than I had signed on to handle. And you'll see we paid for a minimal funeral because Andy, for all his wrong choices at the end, did work well for us all those years."

"Yes, well, like I said, you did more than I would have done on all accounts." There was a pause on the phone before Rafe spoke up again. "Now, about this letter. I'm not going to act on it right now. If we do decide to go ahead with the sale, I will offer it to the Knights but not yet. I need to see just how things look and, well, talk to the men. I hear Walker is in Austin this weekend, Sawyer is at a cattle auction and Jackson has just come in and sat down. I guess, since you aren't going to be here tonight, I'll have dinner with him. Anything I should tell him?"

"I... no, don't tell him anything. There isn't anything not already said."

"Right, so I'll be here the weekend but then I am running to Austin on business. Do you think you could put me up a night? It will be a long day. Then I'll run out to my house to try to remember what it's like to be there again."

"Sure, I'm at the Guild near the office."

"Got it, I'll be there Monday night. What's your room number?"

"One twelve. Call me to make sure I'm here or you could come by the office and pick up the keys."

"What are you doing this weekend anyway?"

"Nothing exciting. I'm going to just settle in. I'm here for a week and then if I don't have a place I like by then, I might stay here for a while. Okay, time to order dinner. Love you and tell... No, never mind."

The tears that flowed so easily right after Jackson had found her were gone, dammed up, causing a drought without relief. He had held her so tightly in his arms on the side of the highway that she thought he would never let her go.

Numbness was her constant companion now, and it was what kept her company on the sofa as she stared out the window of what might have been a beautiful sunset on any other day. But today, it was just another reminder in a world of reminders that she had nothing.

The pounding on the door woke her up in a panic. Who would be banging on her door? She was shaking when she swung her legs off the sofa onto the floor. She looked at the clock. Eight o'clock. It was getting dark. She walked closer to the door when the banging happened again.

"Piper Kay, open this door."

"Jackson?" she asked barely above a whisper.

"Yeah, baby, Jackson. Open up honey. You forgot something."

"What? I didn't leave anything behind that was so important that you would need to bring it all this way."

"Me, baby, you left me behind and I'm hard to lose." Jackson was here? He wanted in? What did he mean that she left him behind?

Didn't he want me to leave him behind?

"No baby, he did not. Open the door, sweetheart. Your new neighbors are getting worried."

"Yes, I bet they are."

She unhooked the chain, turned the deadbolt and finally unlocked the doorknob. She turned the handle, and opened the door to the best thing she'd seen in her life. Jackson, in well-fitting jeans and a shirt that hugged his torso stood in front of her and all she wanted to do was take it all off to touch his skin. But what she did was stand in the doorway and look into his face. He said nothing but opened his arms for her and she didn't hesitate to jump into them, wrapping her legs around his hips and feeling the crush of his lips on hers.

She was moving backwards, but she acknowledged no more than that. Jackson was devouring her lips and now he was moving to the curve of her neck. His hands released her, allowing her to slide to her feet as he entwined his fingers through her hair. Finally, dragging in breath, he tugged her hair, tipping her face up to his.

"We have a lot of things to fix."

"Do we?"

"We do." She tried to lower her head, but he wouldn't allow it. "We have done our best to screw this up and now it's time to put things back together. I love you Piper Kay Gentry, and we are not leaving here until we are good again. You got me?"

"Yes, sir." Her word was spoken in a type of sob.

He kissed her fast and hard. "Good." Releasing her hair and sliding a hand down to grab hers, he led her back to the sofa. "What do you have for food?"

"Nothing, but if you tell me what you want, I'll get it up here in about twenty or thirty minutes."

"What did you eat?"

"Nothing yet. I fell asleep."

"Is that why you didn't answer the door when I knocked normal?"

"Probably. How about a chicken fried steak meal?"

"Make my order a double and that will work." She stared at him. "I'm a hard-working boy," he flexed his biceps to prove it, "and you have to feed me well to keep me that way."

"I'll have salad."

"No, we are going to be here all night so make it a full meal. What you don't eat I'm sure I'll get to later."

He grinned, and her knees almost gave way. She just stared at him as she made the order and then she continued to stare as she sat in a chair near him.

"You act like seeing me is a surprise."

"It is. I never thought I'd see you again."

He sobered. "And that's something we need to talk about. When I got the call from Josie, I thought I would go crazy with fear. I had no idea if anything would happen to you, but my mind played out the worst scenario. I would find you on the highway, dead. My sweet, perfect for me woman gone forever."

He rubbed the back of his neck and stood up suddenly to pace. "When I found you, and ultimately, knew you were safe in my arms I was undone. Then I was pissing angry." He turned to look at her and she could see and feel the anger rolling off him in waves of heat even now. "What the hell were you thinking, putting your life in jeopardy like that? Did you not know you could have died?"

The tears that had refused to come for a week began to slide down her cheeks. She didn't attempt to dry them. "I just wanted to end the mental kidnapping. We were all hostages waiting for something to happen. I forced it to happen on my terms. I took back control."

"At what cost?"

"I've been asking myself that for a week now. I lost you, the ranch, Josie, your brothers, everyone I care about."

"Why didn't you trust me to figure things out?"

"I'm not used to others fixing my problems. That's my job."

"Really? What about trusting me? Believing me? Obeying me?"

"I don't obey, Jackson, I agree on a plan."

"Well, that's going to change too. When we get married you are going to obey me when it is important."

"Married?"

"Did you think that my love was conditional on you doing the right thing all the time, doing as I say, being perfect?"

She shrugged. "But you left me. You left our bed. You stopped talking to me. What was I supposed to think?"

Jackson had the good sense to look a little sheepish. "I was angry and hurt. I should have whipped your ass, and then set things straight right away, but I thought I would get my emotions under control first, while waiting for you to finish all the appointments and interviews. Then we'd sit down and hash it all out. But the longer I waited, the harder it was, and the easier it became to put it off one more day until today. When I came in and saw Rafe, I looked for you. Rafe gave me your letter to him, and when I rushed upstairs I found your letter to me."

"What changed your mind? Why did you come for me?"

"Because I was an ass, and I realized after talking to Rafe that I hadn't fully claimed you. Oh, we played house really well, but there were no ground rules, no parameters, and no goals to work towards."

"None of my other boyfriends needed that."

"And they weren't for the long haul. Baby we are forever and we are different. We need roots. We crave ownership. We've been acting as though this was a rental relationship. Things are going to change. I'm sorry I acted stupid, but I won't any longer."

"I'm sorry, too. I did take us for granted. I took you for granted. It was like a favorite toy I took out when I had time to play. I always expected you to be there until you weren't."

A knock sounded, and Piper moved to answer the door, but sat back down when Jackson gave her his don't-even-think-about-it look. She loved that she still got them.

They settled the dinner at the table and had taken a few bites when there was another knock at the door. Piper didn't even try to get up. She could hear Jackson's voice murmuring for a moment and then he called her.

"Pips, the police want to make sure you are not being hurt."

Piper came to the door with a French fry in her hand. She decided to do her professional persona to deal with them. It took a few moments to convince them she was fine. It went a lot faster once Jackson explained she had put herself in danger on purpose and had nearly gotten herself killed. The officers seemed to understand the situation much better. When they returned to their dinner it was not as piping hot but still good enough to eat without reheating. Jackson ate his meal and the rest of Piper's chicken.

"Now, we need to finish this. Then we can go back to our lives. This is how I see it."

Jackson outlined her leaving her office at the ranch, maybe opening a small branch office in their little town for GWI. Jackson would move in permanently and they would get married sooner rather than later. He would take over the ranch operations, and she would continue working GWI from her off site location.

"Okay. But do I buy out Rafe and Rosie?"

"I think they would like that."

"Me too. We will need a new foreman."

"I've hired Jason Kirkland, the eldest Kirkland boy. He has done a great job and I want to give him a career. Besides he listens to me."

"You hired him without consulting me?"

"You quit, remember?"

"Oh, yeah."

"Now, the only thing that we have left to settle tonight is your spanking and having a lot of make-up sex."

Piper opened her mouth and started to speak but closed it again. She knew that taking Jackson was a package deal, bossy spankings and all. Life without him was more than she could ever contemplate again. It was still so fresh a pain, she shuddered in the remembrance of what her future had looked like not two hours ago.

"Okay."

"Piper, did you say okay?"

"Yes."

"Are you agreeing to the spanking or the sex?"

She took a dramatic breath and let it out. "I'm agreeing to both."

It was Jackson's turn to contemplate the situation. Then he spoke with a confidence Piper hadn't heard recently. "Then go to the bathroom first. I'll wait for you."

Chapter 21

Jackson heard the toilet flush and laid his belt on the couch. Normally he would have made a production of pulling the leather from his belt loops but it had been a big step to accept his way of leveling their world again and put them back on the right track so he didn't want to punish her decision just her ass. He watched her walk toward him and could see the hesitation in her body language.

When she looked at him he could see the trepidation.

"Trust me?"

She stared at him for a few moments before she nodded. "Yes, implicitly."

"That's my baby."

He put his hand out to her and she made the last few steps to him and placed her smaller hand in his. He often marveled at the size difference reminding him she was fragile right now.

He watched her face as he reached up, and unbuttoned the slacks she had on, slowly unzipping the front of them. She bit her lip when he ran his hands down the outside of her thighs, drawing the slacks down with them. He put his hand behind one knee and lifted, bracing her hip as she stepped out of the pants first one leg then the other. He tossed the cloth to the side.

He slid his hands back up the now naked thighs, and hooked his thumbs in the elastic of her panties, and slowly retraced the pathway to the floor. She stepped out of them. He kissed her muff and pulled back.

"It's time."

He helped her over his knee and as she went down she saw his belt. "Jackson, you aren't going to use that, that belt, are you?"

"Mm hmm, but not yet. We have some talking and warming up to do."

"But, I don't want that. I mean, I said okay to your hand, but you didn't say anything about a belt."

"No, but I said leather. This is leather. I forgot to stop in the tack room for your new leather strap. This will have to do. Stings less, but it will get the message across."

Her muscles tightened and there was no doubt his girl was imagining all sorts of retribution. She agreed by actions but not words. This might have been the first time. Jackson appreciated her submission, but he had no intention of going light on his girl. She could have died and all because she was impatient and wanted her way. That was not happening again.

"I hate it when I have time to think about it. Just do it."

Jackson didn't answer in words, but his first sizzling smack positively did not go straight to her clit. Hot damn this sucker hurt. There was nothing sexy about the hard hand peppering every available spot on her ass. She had told herself she would submit to his discipline, that he needed it but she knew she did too. It was the most cathartic thing in her world for those most heinous of personal crimes, selfishness.

Jackson didn't lecture, it wasn't his style but what was his style he had practiced well. Her rear was so hot and the burn was penetrating. Okay, she was handling it okay, she could get through this. The slap on her flank was brutal. She knew there were worse things than Jack's hand but right now, the only thing she could think of was the now obvious rhythmic pattern he was tattooing on her.

Right, right, right, left, right, right, right then reverse. Left, left, left, right…

She squirmed, she wiggled, she cried out and still he continued.

When would he be ready to kiss her pain away and make it blend with her desperate need for his loving? Piper groaned her frustration. She knew he wanted to make sure that they never got to this place again. She wished there were another way. He didn't feel the same.

Jackson had made it clear a long time ago that he hated to repeat a lesson. In his opinion, the way to ensure that he didn't have to was to make the penalty so unforgettable that the next time she thought about crossing his line, the memory of the experience raced to the front of her mind crying *"Warning! Spanking, ahead!"*

All Piper wanted now was a demonstration of love healing all pain. She could endure the lesson if it ended in a renewal of their relationship and his generous lovemaking.

"I get it, Jackson."

"If you had to say it, you aren't there yet. Trust me to know, baby."

Was he right? There would always be her penchant for doing things regardless of the warnings. She had built her reputation on seeing the barriers to success and knocking them out of the way. But this was not worth her bottom's sorrow. She would be better.

The now random swats were not as strident and then all movement stopped. He stopped. Her wiggles and kicking stopped. *Thank God*. Piper relaxed. The sob she'd been holding was released. He'd finished. They could now go on to the loving they both needed.

The healing.

He stood her on her feet holding on as he also rose off the couch. What? No kissing her red achy bottom? No massaging her red globes? No tantalizing her clit? Was this part of her punishment? No loving tonight? That was something she wasn't sure she could handle. Was Jackson still angry despite his words earlier and his discipline?

"Lean over the arm of the sofa, baby. Five with my belt."

"What? Jackson, I can't."

"You can. Listen to me. You very nearly died. You could have been cold in the ground right now. Do you understand how close to losing you I came? How close I came to never sinking deep inside of you ever again? Your mouthy comebacks, your twinkling eyes when you get what you have worked so hard for, your laugh. All gone."

His voice was husky and filled with tears. His eyes were wet and overflowing with the frightening memory.

"I can do this. I promise you that I will never, ever, put myself in such grave danger that it is a real possibility that I could die. I love you too much to do that to you again." Her tears, dried by now, had begun for the second time tonight.

No more words. No more apologies. No more promises. He led her to the arm and leaned her over the hump and before she had time to think he had laid down five mind numbing stripes.

"Never again, Piper. If I have to swat you ten times a day, I will so I never have to discipline you this severely again."

Jackson brought Piper up from her bent position and pulled her into his arms. His tongue caught her tears as they fell. His kisses were tender as they proceeded across her cheeks and along her jawline to finally land on her trembling lips.

"I'm sorry, Jackson, I didn't do it to defy you or to scare you." She sniffled and hiccupped as Jackson lifted her into his arms and sought out the bed in the small suite. "I was trying to make sure everyone was safe. But for the record, ten times a day will never happen."

He chuckled. "Shh, lay your head on my shoulder. You are my perfect woman, and don't ever think I believe any different."

"Do you think I could change the ranch's name to Clearwater Ranch? Maybe we could consolidate?"

"Hush, baby."

He dropped her feet to the floor as he kicked his shoes off walking her backwards. Leaning down, he helped to placed her in the center of the bed. "Clearwater Ranch Daddies. I like it."

"Are you telling me that each of your brothers—"

"Are Daddies. Now stop talking and scoot over, baby cakes."

A mere few hours ago, she had thought never to hear that endearment again. She loved him with every fiber of her being. "I love everything about you, Jackson Knight."

He had stripped his clothes off and stood before her in all his naked glory as he started removing hers. "Thank goodness for that, otherwise I might feel awkward taking advantage of you like I'm about to do."

He pulled the cover back and rolled Piper under it. He joined her, situating her on top of him then reached around to rub her bottom.

"Ow, it hurts, Jackson. It's still tender."

"I hope it remains tender for a good while. Now, about that loving I promised."

"Mmm, yes about that..."

THE END

About the Author
Alyssa Bailey

USA Today Bestselling Author of Sassy Romance that is realistic and sensual with a touch of suspense. A dyed in the wool Texan living in Alaska for half her life, Alyssa now divides her time between the beauty of Southeast Alaska and the piney woods of East Texas. She enjoys taking from her own experiences to create series in fictitious worlds sure to tease the reader's palate and invite them to sink into exciting adventures.

Alyssa enjoys writing consensual power exchanges between intelligent, sassy women who are not afraid to make a stand and loving men confident enough to give his woman space but masterful enough to keep her indulged and protected. There is *always* a happily ever after.

Visit me online and sign up for my Newsletter:
http://alyssabailey.com[1]
Join my Facebook Page for fun and prizes:
https://www.facebook.com/alyssabailey.romance

---

1. http://alyssabailey.com/

Other Books By Alyssa Bailey

Safe and Secure Series: Contemporary, suspense, spicy
    Saving Sharlee
Saving Jessie
Saving Ivy
Saving Mallory
Saving Callie
Saving Becky
Saving Oakley
Saving Finley (2023)

CLEARWATER DADDIES Trilogy -Contemporary, Spicy
    Piper's Plan
Camille's Second Chance
Josie's Refuge

DARLING DUCHESSES: Regency, Daddy Dom, Spicy
    The Devil Duke's Little Distraction
The Daring Duke's Little Impulse

GUARDIANS OF REFUGE (Contemporary, Military, Spicy)

SEAL of Refuge
The Strategy of Love
The Tactics of Love
The Mandate of Love

Sage County (Cowboy, Contemporary, Spicy)
Deep Waters
Still Waters

IN THE SPIRIT OF CHRISTMAS -Contemporary, Sweet
Christmas Wishes and You

ANTHOLOGIES (HEAT VARIES)
Sweet Town Love
Historical Heroes
Hero to Obey (limited time)
Cowboy for a Cause (limited time)
Naughty 12 Days of Christmas 2017

MULTI-AUTHOR BOX SETS (Heat Level Various)
Love, Christmas 2 Recipes
Irresistible Heroes
Sweet and Sassy Summertime Vol. 2
Dear Santa: A Christmas Wish
Sweet and Sassy New Beginnings

Audiobooks
Accepting His Ways
Her Sweet Complication
His Gentle Persuasion
Quinlan's Quest
Lady Caroline's Defiance

These Series will be re-released soon...

Lords and Little Ladies: Georgian Historical, spicy

Chase Abbey Series: Regency, Spicy, Suspense

The O'Connor Series: Contemporary, Rancher, Saga, Spicy

Liam & Jocelyn's Story

Ciarán and Katherine's Story

Quinlan and Cheyenne's Story

Kelli and Parker's Story

Cián and Molly's Story

Lone Wind Series: Contemporary, spicy Native American

Taming Texanna: American Historical, Native American, Spicy

Cowboy Welcome: Contemporary, Spicy

Alyssa Bailey written as Tasha Winters

Coming Soon...

CAPTURED SERIES-URBAN Fantasy/Time Travel
Alphas In The Wild

Don't miss out!

Visit the website below and you can sign up to receive emails whenever Alyssa Bailey publishes a new book. There's no charge and no obligation.

https://books2read.com/r/B-A-MXIL-JZFMC

BOOKS 2 READ

Connecting independent readers to independent writers.

Did you love *Piper's Plan*? Then you should read *Josie's Refuge (Second chance, Daddy Dom book 3)* by Alyssa Bailey!

It started with a trick and now someone may die if they don't eliminate the threat.

Unemployed again, Josie's friend tricks her into accepting a job with the last man she would ever work for, the one she can't forget. With no other choice, Josie decides it's time to deal with her biggest barrier to a happy life, and learn to be vulnerable, but she doesn't know how.

Walker is just as upset as Josie for being duped into offering a job on the sly, but for different reasons. He loves her and wants the best, but if she doesn't learn to accept help, they are doomed in their working relationship and their private one.

Soon, it was obvious Josie was in danger, and the Knights were going to take care of business. Their business.

This book is all about Second Chances, Suspense, and Steamy Love on the Ranch.

Read more at alyssabailey.com.

Also by Alyssa Bailey

Clearwater Daddies
Piper's Plan

Watch for more at alyssabailey.com.